The French Translator

First edition published in 2025
© Copyright 2025
Allison Osborne

The right of Allison Osborne to be identified as the author of this work has been asserted by her in accordance with the Copyright, Designs and Patents Act 1998.

All rights reserved. No reproduction, copy or transmission of this publication may be made without express prior written permission. No paragraph of this publication may be reproduced, copied or transmitted except with express prior written permission or in accordance with the provisions of the Copyright Act 1956 (as amended). Any person who commits any unauthorised act in relation to this publication may be liable to criminal prosecution and civil claims for damage.

All characters appearing in this work are fictitious. Any resemblance to real persons, living or dead, is purely coincidental. The opinions expressed herein are those of the author and not of Orange Pip Books.

Paperback ISBN: 978-1-80424-669-6
ePub ISBN: 978-1-80424-670-2
PDF ISBN: 978-1-80424-671-9

Published by Orange Pip Books
335 Princess Park Manor, Royal Drive,
London, N11 3GX
www.orangepipbooks.com

Holmes & Co. Mysteries

Collection one
The Introduction of Holmes & Co
A Study in Victory Red
The Circle Code Conundrum
The Impossible Murderer
The Happy Family Facade
The Red Rover Society
The Detective's Nemesis

Collection Two
The Adventures of Holmes & Co
The Hidden Case
The Missing Two
The American Visitors
The Dismantled Minds
The French Translator
Return to Baskerville

"To underestimate one's self is as much a departure from truth as to exaggerate one's own powers."

-Sherlock Holmes, *The Greek Interpreter*

Chapter I
A Nervous Man with A Book

Irene Holmes picked up her pace as she turned down Baker Street. Though the crisp autumn air was welcoming, she was eager to get home for the new crossword. The newspaper had hired a new writer for the puzzles a week and a half ago—whomever wrote them was skilled. It was no real challenge, of course, but it did take her an extra moment or two to complete the puzzles, compared to the last writer's efforts.

She tucked a dark curl behind her ear, but it bounced right back against her cheek. Marla—Eddy Lestrade's sister and Irene's former roommate—had just given her a haircut, convincing Irene to chop her locks off at her shoulders. The woman then styled it in a completely different way, curls coiled like copper. While Irene's head did feel lighter, she was very aware of her hair bouncing up and down, her new fringe sweeping across her forehead.

Marla had been over the moon when Irene asked her for a haircut. The woman prattled on and on about some new beau and then begged her not to tell Eddy. Irene barely managed to bite her tongue from saying she wouldn't even remember, let alone care to pass it along to the DI.

She finally arrived at 221 Baker Street. Isla, the young West Highland Terrier, came to the top of the steps and watched Irene take her boots off, but never descended. Her tail, however, wagged furiously.

Irene paused, considered the pup, then noticed the coats. Two of them hung by the door, with two pairs of shoes below. One, the same size as her own, and lined up perfectly under the red jacket. The other, smaller, a child's pair, sat askew under a yellow jacket with one arm stuck inside out.

A client? Possible, though one not in distress—those usually forgot to take their coats off or tossed them in hurry.

There were no voices coming from upstairs.

Curious.

She headed upstairs and into the flat.

A young girl around ten years of age was slouched in Joe's armchair. Her blonde hair needed a brush—or three—and her dark blue eyes blinked up at Irene, holding a thousand questions. She was slight, but still had the round cheeks for her age.

The girl perked up, seemingly the only one in the flat, though Irene was certain she saw Joe's coat hanging on the hook. She wanted to look, but she didn't want to take her eyes off the visitor.

The girl grinned, showing some gaps in her smile. "Hello there!"

She jumped up, crinkled dress falling to her ankles, and took a few steps toward Irene, whose only thought was to back away. Children were hard to read in their actions and this one seemed eager to touch her.

"Miss Hudson!" She yelled, voice cracking as the girl stepped forward again. "Miss Hudson, there is a child!"

"I am not a child!" The girl pouted, folding her arms across her chest and the expression was extremely familiar.

"Yes, you are. Who do you belong to?"

"I belong to no one!"

Before Irene could retort again, the lavatory door banged open. She spun, fists up, though there was no need.

"Who are you?" She snapped at the poor young woman. Her eyes were the same colour blue as the younger one, her hair the same dark blonde, though hers hung in soft waves down her back.

Before the girl could stammer out an answer, footsteps thudded down the stairs from the third level.

Doctor Joe Watson rushed into the living area, a large textbook in his arms. "Irene. It's okay, these—Oh, you've cut more of your hair than you said you wanted."

The younger girl pried the book from Joe's arms as Irene shrugged at his comment.

"Marla was rambling, and I let her do whatever she wanted. Who are—Oh! Of course!"

She almost slapped her palm to her forehead.

How could she forget that Joe's sisters, Alice and Eleanor, were coming today? She had it in her mind that it was next week, though she could've sworn that next week was today's date, instead.

"Hi!" Alice was right beside her, text clutched to her chest. "I have so much to tell you! I was going to write but then Mama reminded me we were coming into London to see you and that I would arrive at the same time as my letter so I decided to just talk to you in person instead!"

Her voice bounced with a lilting northern accent. Joe's own accent had smoothed out a little, but his younger sister's sing-song words flew from her mouth at an alarming rate.

"Have you started the decomposing that I suggested?" Irene asked, tugging off her jacket.

"Oh, yes!" Her hair bounced as she nodded her head. "Three different frogs and—"

"It's so gross," Eleanor chimed in.

Alice rounded on her sister. "It is not! It's science!"

"Science or not, you don't need to keep it in your room!"

Irene opened her mouth to interject, but Joe grasped her arm.

"Let them at it. You won't get a word in edgeways, anyway. Come with me." He tugged her gently toward her bedroom. She had no idea what he could want to speak to her about, and she squirmed away from him as soon as they were beside her bed.

"Is this about my hair?"

"What? No, no."

Irene believed him, but the concern persevered.

Joe seemed just as worried as he spoke. "You forgot my sisters were coming today, didn't you?"

"I did," she said, still tugging on the strands. "I thought it was next week because I do not know what day it is today. Does my hair—"

"It's still okay that they are here for a few days?"

"Of course. This is your house as well, and they are your sisters. Now, please, my hair."

"Your hair looks fantastic," Joe snapped, then collected himself. He ran his long fingers through his own strands, in need of a trim, the auburn curling around his ears. "It compliments your face and draws even more attention to your eyes and your cheekbones, which are lovely."

Irene's cheeks flushed. Even though she'd asked for his opinion and fished for a compliment, his kind answer caught her off guard. She folded her arms across her chest and huffed. "Good. Thank you."

"Also," Joe grabbed her arm again, though Irene had no intention of leaving. "Please don't mention Sarah."

That was peculiar.

Sarah and Joe had been in a relationship going on more than a year now, and though Irene had her opinions on the matter, he kept trudging through the relationship. "Why?"

"Please."

"But why? I don't understand. Do I pretend she simply doesn't exist?"

Joe kept hold of her arm, sighing deeply. "I will attempt to explain myself later, when my sisters have left. Just please don't mention her."

"Okay. She does not exist."

"Thank you." He finally released her and gestured to the door. "Now, tell me your trepidation about your hair, because it does look quite fetching."

She scowled as they left the room. "Marla told me this style is in fashion and, though she is not wrong, I must put curlers in it every night."

Both girls in the room perked up.

Joe wandered over to the small kitchenette and filled the kettle. "You already put curlers in your hair, though."

Irene stopped in front of Alice, who was sitting in her chair, waiting. When she didn't move, Irene shooed her with a flick of her hand. Alice eagerly shuffled off and sat on the floor in front of her, as if a schoolteacher was about to read a story to the class.

"I don't do it every night. How do I curl my hair if it's already curled?"

Eleanor appeared by Alice, skirt hitting her little sister in the face. "I can show you!"

The younger sister pursed her lips in a pout. Irene smiled in amusement.

"Wonderful. The lesson will happen tonight."

In the meantime, Eleanor sat on the couch. "You do have nice hair. Joey was right."

Before Irene could answer, Alice spoke, tugging at her own blond mop. "I hate my hair. I want to chop it all off."

Irene shook her head. "Your round face would do unwell with such a cut, unless you want to look like a boy, of course."

Alice shrugged. "Fine by me. People would actually listen—"

Eleanor didn't let her sister lament. "Do you know much about face shapes, Irene? I thought it related directly to beauty, but does it have other uses? I think my face shape is square. Am I correct?"

"Face shape has many uses. Beauty is one of them, I suppose. You do, in fact, have a square face."

"I knew it."

"That is not a bad thing. You have a petite nose, so if you wanted to cut your hair like a boy, you wouldn't look like one."

The young woman looked like Irene had just slapped her across the face. "I don't want to look like a boy!"

"You wouldn't," Irene said. "Just your hair."

Alice stood, still clutching the textbook. "I want to look like a boy! Can you cut my hair, Irene?"

Joe stepped amongst them, handing out teacups.

"No one is cutting anyone's hair," he said in a soothing, brotherly tone. "Let's finish our tea, then get going."

Irene took her mug from him. "Going where?"

"To the shopping centre, and perhaps Harrods, if they are good."

Joe rarely went out, and when he did, Irene knew about it ahead of time. He usually went to the veterinarian office, or out in the evenings with Sarah, but that was becoming few and far between.

"What happens if we get a case?"

"I will be back in a couple of hours, but no one has contacted us in a week or so."

"That means the probability of someone contacting us is very high."

"Then I'm sure you can entertain them until I return."

* * * * *

Half an hour later, Alice and Eleanor tugged their jackets on, while Irene sat in her chair, debating on whether to go with them. On the one hand, she longed to do something, especially with her hair all done up. But, her chair, and the fire, and a new record Miss Hudson brought home a few days ago beckoned her to stay.

"Last chance, Irene," Joe called from the hallway.

She opened her mouth to tell them to go on without her when the front door rang.

Isla erupted in a fit of barks and bolted toward the hallway. Joe scooped her up as she went past.

From the bottom of the stairs, Miss Hudson's Scottish brogue drifted up, as well as the quiet voice of a man.

She hustled upstairs and urged the group back into the room, waving her strong arms, white hair bouncing as she hurried.

"There is a man at the door asking for you both. Says he has a crime he wants to speak with you about, but not one he committed. He was very clear about that. He's nervous as all get out and he is holding a book as if someone might swipe it."

"A case," Alice squealed. "Can we stay, Joey? Please!"

Eleanor groaned. "I don't want to stay. I want to go shopping!"

Alice glared at her. "We can shop after the case."

"But what if it's a big case? Is it going to be a big case, Joey?"

"I have no idea."

Irene ignored them all and addressed Miss Hudson. "Did you tell him our fee?"

"I did."

"Give us one minute, then show him up." Irene turned to the sisters. "You both may stay if you sit in the corner and be quiet."

"Okay!" Alice skipped away to Irene's desk and sat on the chair, flinging her jacket as she went.

Joe stepped closer to Irene. "We don't know what the man wants. What if it's something…inappropriate?"

"Then we shall send them out," Irene answered a little too loud.

"Oh, please don't send us out!" Alice cried.

"Then sit and be quiet."

With confirmation that they really were staying to see this case, Eleanor trudged to Joe's desk and flopped in the chair.

Meanwhile, Joe set Isla down and shrugged off his own jacket while Miss Hudson went to fetch their guest.

The man that entered a few moments later looked as if the sirens blared overhead. His eyes darted left and right behind round spectacles, and his coat hung too loose on him. His moustache was frayed at the ends, as if he'd played with it too much. He clung to a book as if removing it would kill him.

Irene sat in her chair as the man handed their fee to Joe, to which he stuffed in the back of his notebook.

Their visitor hesitated before sitting, glancing at Joe's sisters.

Irene snapped her fingers, jolting the man's attention to her.

"Pay them no mind and please start talking, Mr…"

He still hesitated, then at her raised brow, started into his story.

"Hubert. My name is Hubert Renaux. I…I am a translator, you see," his accent had a French lilt. The man fiddled with his glasses then his sleeve, the book still clutched to his chest. "French mostly, but I can speak some Italian, though I don't advertise that too much these days."

He dragged a handkerchief from his pocket to wipe his brow.

"You've obviously translated something that's troubled you," Irene said. "So, let's hear it."

He didn't seem too taken aback by her abruptness. In fact, he seemed eager to not have to talk about himself anymore.

"This book—more of a personal diary, really—was anonymously donated to a museum. It's what the curators love for; a look into history, if you will. They are always more of a joy for me to translate than academic papers. However, you don't get this kind of trouble with papers about rocks—"

"Mr. Renaux. Please. What's in the book?"

"Secrets, Miss Holmes. Dark secrets."

She held out her hand, but the Frenchman shimmied away. Irene bit back an insult and looked at Joe.

"Mr. Renaux, we—"

"I didn't write it," he stuttered. "I want you to know. I didn't write it, and I haven't gone to look at any of the places or anything."

Irene waved her hand. Renaux hesitated, but then slowly released his grip, holding the book out to her. She snatched it as soon as it was within reach.

"I didn't write—"

"Of course you didn't write this," she said as she flipped through the pages. "You are clearly left-handed. This was written by a right-handed man with a bad habit of smoking cheap cigarettes and using very expensive pens. And had a short-haired cat."

The book was entirely in French, and Irene couldn't even make out one word of the text. "What does it say?"

Hubert rung his hands.

"Did you come here for help or to simply see the inside of our flat?" Irene snapped.

Behind them, Alice giggled.

Irene hid her smile, though the girl's reaction was refreshing. She was used to Joe and his scowl, not an audience who appreciated her veiled threats.

Finally, the man took off his glasses and pinched the bridge of his nose.

"It's a confession, of sorts. It tells where multiple bodies are buried, and where certain funds went. It is a criminal's diary and I want no part of it."

"Why not just return it to the museum, then?"

"Because they may never employ me again if I refuse to translate this. I don't have many other skills, and with all the young women learning French nowadays, I'll soon be out of a job."

Joe leaned forward, pen at the ready to take more notes. "So why not go to the police? Why come to us?"

"Because what if they think I did it? Or think I went and took some of this money? Or, what if the people who wrote this – Gangsters, no doubt — followed me and think I told Scotland Yard all their crimes? That simply wouldn't do! I came here as soon as I realized I could get into trouble."

"Came right here? How did you know about us?"

Hubert wrung his hands again, pushing the skin around his knuckles. It was a few moments before he spoke again. "Sherlock Holmes helped my mother solve a case of her own. I thought it was he who still resided, but the landlady—"

"Miss Hudson."

"Right, she told me that it was his daughter who ran the business now," he turned to Irene. "And that you were just as good; that I could trust you."

Irene nodded at the compliment. "You can trust us, but you can also trust the police, or at least a particular DI we know."

"I'd rather just say I was robbed and start on another project."

"And the museum would accept this?"

"Yes."

Irene raised a brow.

He sighed again. "If I told them what it was, they would have me keep translating it, and probably get the police involved anyway. Then it's on record that I was helping. If I give this to you, then it's not my problem anymore."

Irene glanced at Joe, though the outcome of this conversation was obvious.

"The papers at the back here are the translations?" Irene sifted through them, answering her own question.

"As much as I dared to translate. I am trying to forget what I read."

Irene tried to keep the amused smirk from her face. "You think that these criminals are going to come after you? How would they even know you had the book if it was donated to a museum? Perhaps this was all fiction, written as prose to one day be published as an experimental novel?"

"Because the places in the book are real."

From behind them, Eleanor spoke. "Charles Dickens wrote about London in Oliver Twist, and London is not fictional, but the character is."

Renaux, instead of responding, looked at Joe, seemingly thinking he was the rational one of the group.

"The book is yours now. If you want the rest translated, someone else will have to do it, but…"

"Finish your thought," Irene urged.

"It is in a specific dialect of French. You would need to find someone who can speak that dialect."

"Or you could keep translating it for us."

He shook his head and stood. "No. It is yours now. I am sorry to leave it with you, but surely if they come looking for me, you can tell them I am innocent."

Joe let out a guffaw. "If the gangsters come looking for *us*, you mean?"

Irene picked at her thumb, now anxious to read the translations and find out what made this man so jumpy. She stood to match Mr. Renaux.

"If you are not willing to translate for us, then we have nothing more to discuss. If you change your mind, however, we would welcome the help. Doctor Watson will see you out."

While Joe led the man to the door, Irene went to the dining table and laid out the book and pages of translations.

Alice was at her side in an instant. "What's it say?"

"I will wait for your brother to return before I narrate."

Mr. Renaux hadn't gotten very far into the diary, but what he had translated made Irene practically giddy.

Joe wasn't a foot into the door when Irene waved him over.

"This first entry tells of bodies buried."

"Really?" the younger sister piped up.

Joe steered her away. "Go tell Miss Hudson that our guest has left and that we will have lunch here."

"So, no shops?" Eleanor asked.

"No shops," Irene confirmed. "I require Joe here, as now we have a case!"

"What case?" Joe asked. "Mr. Renaux wants no more part of it, and to be frank, I feel bad for taking his money."

"I do not. We must solve the case of the bodies! Of who wrote this diary!"

"Irene, there is no case. Let's give the book to Lestrade and all go out for a nice dinner with the money. In fact, why don't you take the book to Scotland Yard and I will take the girls out shopping—"

Alice spoke. "I want to go to Scotland Yard with Irene!"

"No," Joe said, then scolded his sister when she stomped her foot. "Don't pout."

"These coordinates are not far out of the city," Irene continued, unruffled. "We can investigate and still be home for dinner."

Joe was already shaking his head. "You can't simply exhume bodies."

"You can't in a graveyard, but if we are digging holes in random spots in the ground and stumble upon a body, that is different."

"Can I come dig up bodies?" Alice spoke from behind Irene.

"Of course—"

"Not." Joe cut her response.

The girl stomped her foot again. "If I'm to be an investigator one day like Irene, then I need experience!"

Joe pointed at her toes, tapping impatiently. "Not with the attitude you're giving me right now. I'm tempted to send you home just for that."

She stuck her bottom lip out.

"And you," he turned to Irene. "We will go dig, if only because you won't let it rest until we do, or you will go yourself and get in trouble. But once we're done, we turn that book over to Lestrade and come home. Is that clear?"

For a moment, the air in 221b Baker Street stood perfectly still.

Irene felt the girls' eyes on her as she stared at Joe. She'd seen and heard Joe get firm with clients and scoundrels alike, but never had he sounded more like a parent—or a stern older brother—than now.

Surprisingly, she didn't argue back. A firm and bold Joe was something she was quite fond of, so she kept her mouth shut.

Joe must've realized his tone, because red crept up his neck, but Irene turned his sisters before he could apologize.

"There is nothing to be learned by simply digging. We shall relay everything we find when we return. Besides, a group of people wandering around an area, digging up bodies, is sure to be noticed. Perhaps Miss Hudson will take you to that shopping centre or Harold's."

"Harrod's," Eleanor corrected.

"That one too." Irene turned to Alice. "I promise you shall be part of this case if it warrants your scrutinizing eyes. But for now, we shall find out exactly what we're dealing with."

At first, she thought the girl might protest again. Joe was eyeing her, whether he was surprised or not she couldn't tell, but she waited for Alice's answer. She had no idea what she would do if the young girl objected, though.

Pouting profusely, Alice nodded at last.

"Okay. Promise me you'll tell me everything when you return?"

"We will tell you what we can." There was no way she was making a promise to tell Alice *everything*, in case there was something that ought not to be shared yet—not even when Irene hadn't had time to figure things out.

Alice flopped on the couch, but Eleanor looked quite happy to be going on a potential shopping trip.

With the girls settled, Irene plucked her jacket from the hook, book firmly in her grasp. "Come, Joe. We have work to do."

As she left the flat to find Miss Hudson and give her instructions, she heard him say some final words to his sisters before he joined her.

Chapter II

The Concerns of a Frenchman

Joe navigated using the map in his lap as Irene turned down another road. The translations were word for word, but the prose wasn't that exciting.

"A collection of men are buried. Ones I had ordered dead," He read out loud. Indeed, this would not receive any accolades for wordsmithery. He read the coordinates and a crossroad outlined after.

Nevertheless, a case was exciting—and needed, as they both grew restless without something to do. Joe had even reduced the time he spent at the veterinarian practice. Though his career guaranteed a steady and decent income, and the work was rewarding, there was something thrilling about investigating and travelling all around the city; or in this case, just outside the city limits. He'd grown to love the work, and considered himself an investigator first, and a veterinarian second.

However, guilt churned in his stomach as they grew closer to their destination. Today, when his sisters were visiting, was not the day for a case, no matter how interesting. But he couldn't say no to Irene, or his commitment to their business.

As they left London behind, he sighed.

"Perhaps I should send my sisters home, as I fear this case may take a dramatic turn."

"Why?"

"Because all our cases do."

"Hm. I suppose so. That's the nature of the game, though."

"I was really excited for you to spend some time with Alice." Scenarios ran through his mind. He'd pictured Irene and Alice getting along and sharing stories, perhaps getting Eleanor involved as well.

"I had considered bringing her," Irene said. "But I saw your worry, and the points I made were valid. Alice is whip-smart, but still young and excitable. Exactly how I was. As much as my father used to let me help and would bring me along, looking back, he knew when to leave me with Miss Hudson, because the subject matter was too dark or dangerous, or because I would simply be a nuance."

"She just wants to solve a mystery. If I could find a simple one for her, then she'd be the happiest girl in the world."

"Perhaps this one will be simple. A journal that tells of a shooting. Wrapped in a nice little bow, no matter how dramatic that translator was. Let's see what we find. We can always give her the illusion that she is helping. Plus, once this case is over, we can go through some of the old cases together, or some of my father's cases, or even some new things we pick up along the way."

Joe smiled at his partner. "I appreciate your help with her, Irene. It's a bit unlike you, but it's appreciated all the same."

"A bit unlike me? To what? Help? Be thoughtful of others?"

He tried to find a joke in her tone, but there was none.

"Oh, Irene! Sorry. That's not what I meant."

"I know," she said, smirking at him. "I never wanted siblings. And I was always worried Uncle John would have kids of his own someday, lest the attention be taken off me."

"Have you changed your mind after seeing me with my sisters?"

"Absolutely not."

* * * * *

"There," Joe pointed. "The church."

Irene pulled to the side of the road at the edge of a woods. The trees had all but lost their leaves from the autumn chill, and though the branches were bare, the forest went deep and uphill.

"I'm glad we are here during the day. This place would be downright eery at nighttime."

Irene climbed out of the Vauxhall. "We've been to worse."

Joe grabbed two shovels out of the back of the automobile. "We've also been to better."

A hole was blown out of the side of the church. Bricks and stone were strewn around the foundation, but the pews inside were still intact. While Joe wasn't religious, seeing yet another church destroyed by the war tugged at his heartstrings.

"Thirty paces, correct?" Irene asked, poised at the cornerstone of the dilapidated building.

Joe flipped open his notebook. "Thirty paces, then turn enough to see the both the church and the tree with the face in it."

They navigated through the trees until they'd counted their paces, then pivoted slowly.

"Got it," Joe said. The broken spire of the church caught on his left side, and just to his right was a gnarly tree with bark that twisted into a sad face.

Irene stomped around, testing the ground, before giving a cry of delight. "Soft ground!"

She stuck the shovel in the dirt and started digging. Joe started on his own hole near her. Thankfully, the temperature had stayed warm enough that the ground had yet to freeze and turn hard. Still, digging was not an activity that brought any sort of joy.

Occasionally, his brain still flashed to the war; from digging foxholes for cover to burying bodies. Nowadays, those flashes were a distant memory. His life had drastically changed for the better, after all. Yet sometimes the memories surged forward as if the war had been just yesterday.

On those rare occasions, Joe looked to Irene, usually babbling away about some case, or fungi, or word origin. His panic usually dispelled immediately.

Luckily, no flashes came to Joe now. After a solid ten minutes, he'd removed his jacket and rolled up his sleeves. Sweat beaded his forehead and an angry vein snaked up his arm.

Irene was just as sweaty and unkempt. Her nose ran from the chilly air and she kept wiping her face on her sleeve like a child.

"What if digging is a waste of time?" he grunted. "What if—"

A crunch beneath his shovel.

Joe immediately dropped the tool and crouched. Irene was beside him in a second, on her knees, brushing away the dirt. A dark grey bone, cracked from the shovel, lay in the hardened ground.

They both dug and brushed furiously, uncovering bone after bone. Joe stood and grabbed his shovel again, widening the area while Irene worked close to the discovery, uncovering the detail.

Within half an hour, both breathless, backs and hands throbbing with pain, they had uncovered three bodies, rotted down to the bones. The skeletons lay face down side by side.

Some cloth and tissues were scattered around, the rest lost. The scent of death was long gone, replaced by hearty, healthy earth and dust.

"This one had a broken wrist," Irene said, pointing to the middle body. "This one, a broken femur."

"Irene. Look at their heads."

The skulls were all still intact, though one had a broken jaw. But all three had the same hole in the back of their head.

Irene leaned closer before gently lifting a skull. Metal rattled around and fell out of the eye socket to the dirt below.

The bullet was a rumpled ball bearing from a small calibre weapon. She pointed to the other two bodies, but Joe was already rooting around the dirt. He found the other two bullets and dropped them in Irene's hand.

"Do we go to Lestrade?" His stomach churned as it finally realized he'd just pushed aside two human skulls.

Irene stared at the bodies. "We have nothing for him but a diary and three skeletons."

"True, but what if that book holds more secrets like this? What if we've stumbled upon someone's murder confessions? What if these are unsolved missing people?"

"They were executed."

"Exactly. These could be anyone."

Irene crouched to the bodies once more. "We need Mr. Renaux back to translate the rest of that diary. But first, we shall go to Eddy, if only because I want these bodies processed and files started. Then others can do the legwork of researching the identities so we can focus on the important things."

"Like whom wrote this diary."

"Precisely. I assume it's a dead man writing his confessions. But these are dangerous words and serious crimes. I wouldn't be surprised if someone was out looking for this donated work."

"Perhaps," Joe offered, attempting to see a better, lighter side of things, "they donated the diary so the crimes would come to light and the author would be exposed for his criminal behaviour."

"Oh, Joe," Irene clasped his shoulder. "You have such a positive outlook."

"And you always have a negative one."

"And who is correct most often?"

"You are."

"Correct." She patted his arm.

* * * * *

As Irene pulled to the side of the road near Scotland Yard, Joe brushed his jacket. They were both dirt-covered and looked like they'd clearly either dug a base for a house or exhumed several bodies.

Scotland Yard had grown twofold in the past year. It had kept some intelligence divisions left from the war, adding a slew of fresh faces and job positions. Uniformed constables, Detective Inspectors in their suits, and secretaries on their afternoon break made for a crowd humming around the large, gated entrance to the building. Most of them knew Joe and Irene by now, but it still didn't stop them from eyeing the pair.

True to her nature, as soon as they were through the front door, Irene aimed straight for the back offices. Joe tucked his jacket close to himself as they weaved in and out of the desks on the way back to DI Lestrade's office.

His door was closed, and from what Joe could see through the small window, the Inspector in question stood in the middle of the room, looking at a folder. He spun, ready to confront the trespasser, when Irene burst in.

"Easy Eddy," Irene laughed. "You really mean to fight me?"

He smacked her with the folder. "Usually, people knock."

"Do people usually come to you with three executed bodies?"

Joe stepped forward, stretching his hand to Lestrade. "So sorry. We should ask if you have a moment to discuss something."

The DI clasped his hand, then glanced at Irene, who interjected before he could even open his mouth. "Of course he has time."

Lestrade stepped around her to shut the office door. "I have some time, but just a moment. Unless you did, in fact, say something about bodies?"

Irene didn't wait for an invitation before sitting in the chair at the desk. Wasting no time, she told of the translator, handing over the book as she did, and of them digging up the bodies.

"Oh, Irene…" Lestrade sighed. "Why didn't you call me *before* you dug up the bodies?"

"Because I didn't know if bodies would be there. Besides, we are here now."

"I suppose. There might be tellings of other crimes in this book, then? Is that what you're saying?"

"Yes."

"I don't even know if I have time to take this on. Perhaps—"

"If you even suggest talking to another DI, I will take the book back and not tell you anything more."

"I was merely going to suggest Gregory."

Irene huffed. "He wouldn't be the worst, but I want the majority of this case. I only need a DI to make official arrests should they be needed."

Eddy glanced at the stack of folders on his desk. "Translate the rest and come back to me before you do anything else. I will leave the bodies for now. I'm not opening a file for a case that might not go anywhere. However, if those bodies line up with anything more in that book, then I will jump in."

"Excellent. We shall seek out the translator at once."

"Seek out? Do you not know where he is?"

Irene shook her head. "He didn't want any part of the book after he read about the bodies, so now we have to find him and get him to translate the rest."

Lestrade's phone rang sharp and loud, interrupting their conversation. "DI Lestrade speaking."

Irene and Joe turned to leave, but Lestrade snapped his fingers, stopping them.

"They are right here, in fact. Let me get you them." Lestrade held out the receiver to Irene.

Joe's thoughts immediately went to worry and he tucked in close to listen.

"Lucky I got you, Hen," Miss Hudson didn't sound too worried, but there was a hurry in her voice. "There's a man here, maybe from the government, as he has two giant friends outside. Nice enough, though."

"A colleague of Mr. Cullen?" Irene asked.

"Didn't say, Love. Just that he was here for a book that you have. He may be prettier than Mr. Cullen, I will say that, but he speaks a bit funny."

"Speaks funny how?"

"Oh, I'm no good with accents, but I do believe it's French. He's got quite some rings on his fingers, too. A real looker."

"We'll be right there." Irene handed the receiver back to Lestrade. "Keep this."

Meanwhile, Joe's heart thrummed in his chest, threatening to cover his hearing. He had one hand on the doorknob out to Scotland Yard, waiting for Irene to follow.

The DI reluctantly took the book. "What is going on, Irene?"

"There is a man at Baker Street who wants that book. If he's that pressed for it, then he can come to Scotland Yard."

"I'll come with you." The DI grabbed his coat.

"No, Eddy."

Joe tapped his foot. "This man sounds dangerous, Irene."

"Why? Because he has rings and men outside?"

"He has men with him?" Lestrade exclaimed. "Then I am definitely coming with you."

"No," Irene snapped at the both of them. "Joe and I will return to Baker Street and see what he wants. We will tell him we have just left the police station, so he knows that we have friends on the force, and we will tell him we left the book with you. There is nothing he can do to us at Baker Street."

With that plan in place, she breezed past Joe and out the door.

* * * * *

The drive to Baker Street stretched on for ages. Joe's leg bounced so much, he was sure he'd get a cramp. Irene had assured him that Miss Hudson wouldn't let anything happen to his sisters, but he worried anyway.

Irene parked the Vauxhall and Joe leaped out before the engine was even cut. He burst through 221, leaving the front door swinging in his wake. By the time he made it to the top of the stairs, he paused to catch his breath.

Irene caught up to him, but he continued to the flat. He flung the door open, ready to jump in front of his sisters.

The man sitting on the sofa was not much older than Joe himself, with dark, thick hair and matching facial hair. His eyes were bright, either green or blue, but there was something in them Joe instantly distrusted.

Alice sat at Irene's desk, a scowl on her face, as if this visitor had interrupted some important work she was doing. Eleanor, however, sat in Joe's chair, eyes the size of saucers and a smile on her face, gaze glued to the man on the couch.

Joe's ears heated in anger. He needed his sisters away from this man before Alice bit him and Eleanor proposed to him.

The visitor, however, only had eyes for Irene as she stepped in. He stood, fixing his sharp icy stare on her, addressing her with a thick French accent.

"Ah, Mrs. Holmes, you have something that belongs to me."

"We have never met, so that can't possibly be true," Irene responded, her own tone just as cutting.

As usual, she forwent the correction to her title. Joe still didn't know why, but this wasn't the time to dwell on it.

The Frenchman narrowed his eyes. "Oh, but it is true. Please, sit. I don't want to keep you standing in your own home."

Irene strode around the furniture with all the confidence in the world and perched on her chair. Joe was a little more cautious, attempting to read the man before sitting across from him.

He did have rings, just as Miss Hudson said, and though Joe didn't know much about fashion, the Frenchman's clothes seemed well-made and tailored to perfection.

Joe grasped Eleanor's arm and gently guided her away from his chair, then motioned for Alice to follow. To his surprise, his sisters didn't argue. The young girl shot one last glare at the man before following her sister out the door.

As if that was Irene's cue, she crossed one leg over another and folded her arms. "Either introduce yourself or tell us what you want."

He pursed his lips in a smile, still not acknowledging Joe. He was confident, and his age and scarred knuckles hinted that he'd fought in the war—for France, most likely. Which meant years of brutal fighting.

He leaned back and sighed, gesturing to Irene. "I am, how you say…intrigued by you. Doing a man's job of investigating."

Irene ignored the slight. "How did you find me?"

The man smiled. It reminded Joe of a cat spotting a mouse.

"I have my own ways of doing detective work, Mrs. Holmes." He sighed and gestured to her again. "You have two diaries that belong to my family that I require be returned to me."

Irene shrugged. "I do not."

He regarded her for a moment and Joe leaned forward, hoping to catch the man's attention. And yet he still ignored the other male presence in the room, continuing to talk only to Irene.

"I know, for a fact, Mrs. Holmes, that you do."

"There was one handed to us, and it is with the police now," she said. "You may go to Scotland Yard to retrieve it. Or…" Her last word caught his attention. "You can tell us who wrote it."

He laughed. "You are being… What is the word? Hostile toward me."

"You show up at my house dressed like you have important business, showing off rings that don't even belong to you, as they are too big for your fingers. You try to intimidate me and yet you don't."

"If I may say back," he fiddled with one of the ill-fitting rings, "your attitude tells me you know of the contents of the book."

"I do not," Irene lied. "I only know a man trying to intimidate, leaving two men outside an old lady's flat as a scare tactic. And refusing tea."

"How would you know that?"

"Miss Hudson always offers tea, and regardless of the answer, she always brings it. But your refusal must have been quite something that she did not even attempt to bring up a pot."

He smiled again. "You will retrieve my books and return them to me."

"Like I said, there is only one, and it's at Scotland Yard—"

"Because you sent it there."

Joe tensed even more. Irene looked ready to take a swing.

"I will be nice and give you until morning. You will meet me for breakfast at oh-nine-hundred at the Savoy Hotel and return my book."

The Frenchman stood, not abruptly, but quick enough that Joe was on his feet in an instant. He glanced at Joe, gaze flickering up and down, before turning back to Irene.

"Good evening."

Irene stayed in her chair, watching the man head for the door. Joe, however, followed him out, but he never looked back, striding down the stairs and out the front door.

Joe stayed at the top of the steps for a moment, not quite sure what happened was real. He'd been invisible. Not even a second thought given to him.

Footsteps running up the stairs snapped him from his reverie as his sisters barrelled toward him, questions flying at his head.

"Who was he?" Alice asked. "I didn't like the look of him."

"His accent was dreamy," Eleanor fawned. "Like a film star!"

"He was odd, not dreamy, and had a wicked look about him."

"He's just a Frenchman! I bet he's been to Paris!"

"Yeah, to murder someone!"

"Oh, hush!"

Used to his sisters' banter and bickering, Joe simply turned to head back to the flat.

Irene paced back and forth, hands clasped behind her back, thoughtful but with a pep in her step.

"Irene," Joe said as his sisters tumbled in behind him. "This just turned—"

"Exciting! Oh, Joe. This man gave us so much!"

Eleanor pushed past her brother. "What did he give you? His name? Where he was staying? His marital status?"

Joe opened his mouth to chastise her, but Irene beat him to it.

"He is a gangster and a dangerous man, you silly girl."

Eleanor let out a squeak, and Alice laughed at her.

"However," Irene continued, "his good looks do help with his career choice, no doubt."

Eleanor stuck her tongue out at Alice. "Do you always work with such handsome men?"

Joe, already tense from that meeting, and burdened with worry about his sisters, finally snapped at poor Eleanor.

"Is that all you think about? I brought you to the city to gain an opinion on the rest of the world, and all you can think about is men." He knew it was unfair, especially to yell at her in front of Irene and Alice, but he'd done it now.

Before he could apologize, Eleanor stomped her foot, not unlike her sister did earlier. "What else am I supposed to do if not get married and have babies? All my friends have beaus and I'm stuck on the farm."

"You're not stuck. I'm in the city—"

"You also went to war and are so much older than me, and you have Irene. I have no one and nothing."

Joe's ears grew hot again. This was a whole other conversation for another time—not right after a dangerous man had been at their flat.

Luckily, Irene stepped between them. Joe could've kissed her for relieving the tension.

"I require silence from both of you. This is a trivial conversation and we have other matters to attend."

Eleanor gasped. "It's not trivial!"

"It is," Irene fired back. "You are not going to find the love of your life in a French gangster, or from visiting your brother. You meet people by working and going to the places in whose company you want to keep."

"You met Joey on the street and lived with him before you even knew him!"

"Yes, but I met him while *working*. While out in the world, *not* chasing boys. Doing what I wanted, and what made me happy."

"Well, I don't know what makes me happy!"

"And there is the root of our problem. Good, now to move on."

Tears welled in the girl's eyes. She spun on her heel and scurried from the room.

Joe looked at Irene. "Why?"

His friend shrugged. "She is your sister. You would have a better idea of what makes her happy—"

"No, Irene…" He trailed off. "Never mind. Let me go make sure she's alright, then I will send them both home."

"She will be fine. Perhaps she needed those words. We have bigger matters to attend to. We need that journal back—and to find the translator. It must hold some deeper secrets if that burly man is after it. Perhaps he killed the author? And also, there is a second book? Mr. Renaux never mentioned a second. Do you see how this is exciting?"

"I cannot do any of that until I make sure Eleanor is okay."

Before Irene could argue with him, Joe followed his sister up the stairs. She was slumped on his bed, dabbing her face with a tissue. He sat beside her to comfort her as she sniffled.

"She is right," Eleanor said. "I know she is."

"Perhaps. But she was still harsh."

Eleanor gave a soft giggle. "Just like you say in your letters. Smart and sharp."

A knock came from the door and Joe sighed. Irene didn't wait for an answer before sticking her head into the room.

"I would give you longer to chat, but we've not got the time." She stepped into the room and addressed Eleanor. "When can you be ready to go back out again?"

The young girl looked up at her. "Go out?"

"Yes, I assume you want to fix your make-up, as it has run down your face. If you need better mascara, I have some that is almost waterproof."

Her words were pointed and hurried, but her tone earnest, and Joe bit back a smile.

"Just five minutes. Why?"

"I need to go to Scotland Yard to pick up the diary, and you are to come with me. You will see some of the world we chastised you for not participating in. This is a work trip, though. There will be many constables and DIs, but we are there for you to see what actually happens in the real world; that it is not all handsome men and romantic thoughts. Now, wipe your eyes and get ready."

With that, she left the room.

Joe patted his sister's shoulder. "There, see? It all worked out."

Eleanor straightened. "I can see why you like her. She bosses you around, but in a good way."

He sighed for his umpteenth time that day.

Chapter III
Lunch at The Savoy

As Irene and Eleanor tugged their jackets on to head to Scotland Yard, Alice bounced over to them. "Joey said you're going to the police station. Not fair that I can't come."

"We are," Irene said. "And it's very fair. Despite my father taking me everywhere at a young age, there are some places reserved for those older. However, Joe needs to start on our board, to which you will help him."

"Oh truly? Can I write the notes?"

"No. I will only tolerate mine and Joe's writing on our board. But you may help him collect his thoughts and input whatever you remember from our visitor earlier."

"Okay!"

With Alice satisfied, and Joe given a job, the pair of girls headed into the damp evening air. Irene glanced around quickly, but the Frenchman hadn't left any of his men behind.

They climbed into the Vauxhall, and Irene started the engine.

"Do you drive?" she asked Eleanor.

"Oh, no. Why would I need to?"

"In case you want to go somewhere."

The girl looked at her nails. "I can simply have others drive me."

Irene snorted. "It is not wise to rely so much on others."

"But people offer."

"Because they assume you are still a young, naive girl. Not every offer will be something good, even if it is wrapped in a bow. The world sees you for what you look like immediately. People form impressions and it's very hard to get that impression out of your mind. If you dress like a schoolgirl, then they will treat you as such."

"Is that why you wear trousers all the time?"

"I dress like this so people will not think I am a silly girl playing detective."

Eleanor thought for a long moment—so much that Irene thought she'd insulted her.

"If I dress differently, then people will assume I am smarter than I am," she said, picking each word carefully. "Alice is the smart one."

"That doesn't mean you can't also be intelligent."

"People don't look at me for my intelligence."

"Well, you do not drive, you drool over men, and you fling your emotions all over the place as if they were a toy."

"I suppose you are right. Though you don't have to be so harsh about it."

"No, I don't, but sometimes I don't know how to be gentler." She felt Eleanor's eyes on her.

"Are you gentler with Joey?"

"He has stayed at Baker Street with me for almost two years, so I would assume I have not insulted him too terribly."

The girl was quiet for the rest of the short ride and, for a brief moment, Irene worried. However, her thoughts didn't linger on Eleanor long, as she was eager to get the diary back and figure out the rest of the translations.

Joe's sister stuck close to Irene as they headed into Scotland Yard. A Friday evening was both the best and the worst time to be in the police station. There were already a few drunkards yelling at each other, and a woman hysterically crying over her missing son. A few young constables whistled at Eleanor as they passed, and after the third one, she hunched her shoulders, clearly now hating the attention.

"They are all staring at us," she said.

"Yes," Irene led her through the desks. "They will stare, say inappropriate things, and try to touch you. And those are just the police. Most regular men are worse."

They made it to Eddy's office and, as bad luck would have it, Thomas Gregory, in all his slicked glory, stood in the middle of the room, sipping on a cup of coffee. He saw Irene coming and braced himself, then he saw Eleanor behind her.

"And who might you be?"

"Joe's sister," Irene said, in hopes of warding him off.

"Thom Gregory," he stuck his hand out. "You cannot be Joe's sister. You are too beautiful."

Eleanor giggled.

"She's sixteen. You do anything more than shake her hand and I will have Eddy arrest you."

"Oh relax, Irene," he gently chuffed her cheek. "Merely just an introduction."

"And if your hand gets close to my face again, I shall remove it from your body."

"I'm sure you will," he chuckled, showboating in front of Eleanor, but Irene caught the momentary fear and worry that crossed his face.

"We're here to see Eddy, not you."

"A shame."

As they waited, Thom shuffled papers and Eleanor stood perfectly still. To the young woman's credit, all she offered the

DI was a polite smile, though if her fidgeting hands and slight rocking on her heels were any indication, she wanted to flirt and chat with him. But she didn't, and Irene was ever grateful. She gave herself—and the pep talk to Eleanor in the car—all the credit.

Eddy eventually arrived and shook hands with Eleanor before shooing Thom away. Irene dove right into the situation at hand.

"So now, you want the book back?"

"Yes," she said. "But should anyone come in looking for it, it's still here, in a back office or wherever you see fit to lie."

"Is this Frenchman going to come for it?"

"Doubtful, as he seemed the type to stay away from law enforcement, but who can know?"

"You can," Eddy pointed at her. "You know everything."

"Ha! While I enjoy the flattery, I will reserve that compliment for tomorrow when we've met with him."

"Do you need me there?"

"No."

He sighed. Irene counted that as the sixth sigh she'd heard in the past twenty-four hours.

"*Should* I be there?"

Again, she shook her head. "Until we find out more, it shall just be me and Joe that meet with him."

Eleanor turned to her. "What will Alice and I do tomorrow morning, then? Joey promised us—"

"Inconsequential at this moment and to be figured out by your brother later. Right now, we shall take this book and be off."

"Irene." Eddy reached out and caught her arm. "This doesn't seem dangerous right now, but my gut is telling me to tell you to be careful."

"I always am, Eddy."

"No, you're not."

"It will be fine. Come, Eleanor."

The pair exited Scotland Yard with only a few whistles their way. As they drove home, Eleanor appeared dejected and tired, and looked like Joe usually does, slumped in the seat ready for a sleep. They entered the flat, and the girl mumbled a goodnight before heading upstairs to Joe's bedroom.

"Don't wake Alice!" Joe called after her, then turned to Irene. "What did you do to my sister?"

Irene shrugged and handed him the book. "The glamour and mystique of men wore off quickly standing in Scotland Yard for more than five minutes."

"Oh, no. Were they mean to her? Did any of the constables say anything rude?"

"Nothing outlandish, don't fret."

Miss Hudson entered with a tea tray and bid them both goodnight. Irene and Joe started into the tea and late-night sandwiches, both staring at the book on the table.

"She was quite taken by Thom," Irene said, wanting to quell Joe's worry about his sister. "But to her credit, she kept her composure."

"Good. Thom is not the type of man I want her to fall for."

Irene shoved the rest of the sandwich in her mouth. "Not every man she meets is going to be the man she marries."

"It's not just marriage, it's...other things that men want. Relations, and such."

"Ah, and you don't want her to have relations unless she intends to marry."

Joe set his sandwich down and suddenly seemed a man burdened with a thousand tasks. "Yes, I suppose."

Irene sipped her tea. "It's almost nineteen-fifty. The world is changing. Perhaps that should change, too."

Joe picked up the sandwich again, speaking hesitantly. "I don't mean to criticize, and you are the smartest person I know, but I'm not sure how much knowledge you have on this particular topic."

She tilted her head, popping a brow. "You don't think I've spent nights with men?"

Red pooled into Joe's cheeks. "I… Uh…"

She folded her arms. "Well, I have. If only for curiosity's sake. But it's never a whole night. What would I do after? Sleep in their bed? Heavens no. My own is much more preferable."

She grabbed another half sandwich as he stuttered across the table from her.

"Uh… I haven't… When? Actually, I don't wanna… Unless…"

"Don Radcliffe. I met with him before he went back to America."

"Oh."

She shrugged. "It was one evening and to be honest, it was simply okay. Good enough, I suppose."

She was not lying. The man had nice hands, but ultimately, his accent and urgency had put her off enough that she'd refused a second tryst and had returned to Baker Street.

By now, Joe's face was as red as a telephone box. "I think this is better discussed with your girlfriends."

She snorted. "Such as? If I tell Jeannie, she'll give me tips on doing things that I don't want. And if I tell Miss Hudson… Well, could you imagine me speaking to her? But I suppose I don't have to talk to you about this either."

"Well, I mean… If it's something you need to discuss, or have questions, or are concerned…"

He trailed off, and Irene raised a brow again. "It clearly makes you uncomfortable."

"Yes, well…no. I suppose it should if it makes you uncomfortable."

She laughed. "We have discussed much more intrusive things than this. Remember when I had you bring me extra rags for my woman troubles last month?"

He pulled the crust from his bread. "Those are bodily functions."

"So is this." She finished sandwich and eyed his second half.

"Yes, but this is… You're just very vulnerable during… I don't know what I'm trying to say."

"Neither do I. But I can assure you, I have never done anything I didn't want to do."

He stared hard at the table.

Irene was really tempted to snatch his other sandwich.

"Just the thought of men touching you… I dunno."

"Oh, they don't touch me. Not really, and not a lot."

"Then how… You know what, this is a conversation for another day. I need a drink of water before we move on with the case."

"Quite right. The case is severely more important and we must discuss this breakfast tomorrow."

Her words seemed to snap him from his reverie. "We are going?"

"Of course."

He stared at her for a hard minute, and she could see his brain switching conversations. "What are we going to tell him?"

"The truth. I took the book to the police station and they now have it."

"Not the whole truth."

"Of course not." She finally grabbed the sandwich sitting in front of him. "We will hopefully throw him off our scent. Then we must find out who donated those books, and what the rest of the pages say."

"So, we are leaning into this case as serious as ever?" There was hesitation in Joe's words, as if wanting her to throw the whole thing away.

"Even more so."

He sighed, then plucked his sandwich from her hand.

* * * * *

Joe's sisters slept in the next morning, and by the time they both sleepily entered the living area, the pair were ready to leave for their breakfast. He left them with instructions to listen to Miss Hudson before heading out.

The Savoy Hotel was just as nice as The Ritz, and Irene made a mental note to look at the rooms to see if they were on par as well.

The Frenchman was in the restaurant, easy enough to spot at the back corner table. Two large men stood on either side. Even though they weren't close to him, Irene recognised them as bodyguards immediately.

He waved them over in such a curt manner that Irene stiffened, temped to sit at another table and call *him* over. Curtailing that urge, she sat across from him, while Joe took up a seat beside her.

Though his shirt and coat were luxurious, the man's hands were roughened, and a dark blue-black patch sat under the base of his thumbnail. He was handsome, by any right, and his gaze missed nothing, flickering across everything, never stopping to focus, but Irene suspected he processed everything he saw.

"Mrs. Holmes, a pleasure. And you, Doctor Holmes. I don't believe we spoke when I saw you last."

His demeanour was relaxed, as if they were old friends catching up.

"You didn't feel the need to introduce yourself," Irene noted.

"Ah, my apologies," he stuck out his hand. "Andre Barbier."

They both shook his hand. He stuck a cigarette in his mouth and addressed Joe. "Did you fight in the war, Doctor?"

To his credit, Joe stayed calm, facing him head on. "I did."

"How far did you get?"

"Into Germany."

"Well done." He offered the pair a cigarette, but they both turned it down. "I fought too. Made it into Germany myself. When I returned home, there was nothing left of my town, and my family had all come here and brought their businesses. Of course, when London was hit, they did their own hiding. Regardless, I am trying to say that my family's businesses are very important."

"What businesses would they be?" Joe asked.

"Importing and exporting speciality goods."

Irene let out a sharp bark of laughter. "What a business to be in."

"Yes, therefore, I have a certain legacy to uphold."

"As do I."

"I know. I've heard of you, even before I started asking around. And I would like to hire your services."

Irene raised a brow. "I am already on a case."

"I pay better." When she didn't budge, Andre leaned forward. "I know you still have the diaries. I want them back."

"That's why you want to hire us?" Joe interjected.

He chuckled. "No, no, Doctor. You're going to give me my books back if I hire you or not. I want to find the person who took them and donated them to the museum."

Irene shook her head. "Like I've said, there was only one diary, and I'm not going to work for you."

"But you will. You've already translated a portion."

"How would you know anything about what I've done?"

"How do you think I found you? The thin man. Quick to scare."

She felt Joe stiffen beside her. "Where is the translator?"

He shrugged. "I do not know. Truly. He could be at home."

"Or buried six feet under."

"I would have no idea how he got there," he said, then switched the conversation. "Work for me. I pay well, and you have to bring me my books, anyway."

She folded her arms. "You've been cryptic, which does not bode well if you want me to work for you. I don't even know who wrote the book, or who donated it, or where this mysterious second book you're referring to is."

"I have an idea of who gave up the belongings. I need you to find them."

"I am no sniffer dog. You want them found, send one of your men."

Andre shook his head, eyes darkening. "No. You already know part of what is in this diary. It belongs to my family. It's, how you say, sentimental."

Irene stared at him. She didn't want to give up the book at all, as there was a mystery to be had. If this man wanted it back so badly, then there was even more inside those pages.

And yet, did she want to associate with someone who wasn't wholly following the law on any given day?

"Who wrote the book? Whose journal is it?"

"My father's," Andre said without hesitation.

She hated the smug smirk that dressed his lips.

"Then your father is a criminal."

"He's dead, so he will be on trial by God."

She was well aware that Andre knew he had her. She should walk away from this whole mess, but the intrigue drove her wild.

"Allow me a moment to consult with my partner." She stood and motioned for Joe to follow her to the side of the room. Once they were out of earshot of Andre and his men, Joe spoke.

"Are you insane?"

"We have to figure out a way to get everything we can out of that book."

He touched her arm, capturing her attention. "Are you seriously entertaining the idea of working for him?"

"Of course I am. I can extract any amount of money I want. It will pay our way through winter."

"I don't like him."

"Neither do I. He's slipperier than a water snake, but I fear he will hunt this book down."

"So give it to him and let's move on."

"You're not intrigued?"

"No."

"Not one bit?"

"Not at all."

"You're lying."

"Oh, Doctor!" Andre called.

Joe bristled and turned to him.

"You and your wife are running out of time."

Irene slowly started back to the table, deliberately commanding the room. "We want double our upfront fee, and any expense occurred must also be covered."

"Done."

"And you will give us any and all knowledge we require about this diary."

"Only which you need. And in turn, Mrs. Holmes, you will not go to the police, nor will you ask for their assistance. I have plenty of men who will help you should you need to question someone or get in to somewhere."

"I have my own methods for questioning," she smirked as she leaned on the back of the chair. "Now, our fee, and any information you can tell me."

"You will get half now, and the rest along with all the information I have to offer, when you return those books. You will meet me back here for lunch in two hours. That should give you enough time to retrieve what's mine. My men may follow, or they may not. Can I trust you, Mrs. Holmes?"

"No. But you can trust in the fact that I want to solve this."

"That is as good as any promise."

"And what if I truly don't have the book?"

"Then you have two hours to find it."

Chapter IV

The Case Turns Dangerous

Joe needed to get his sisters somewhere safe. But first, he needed to get Irene away from Barbier. She looked ready to go toe-to-toe with him, or befriend him just to figure out what sort of criminal enterprise he ran.

He grasped her arm. "Traffic will be hellish this time of day."

That broke the staring contest.

The pair left the Frenchman and his men in the restaurant. As they drove back to Baker Street, Joe wiped his palms on his trousers.

"I think I will send my sisters home. Which will make them furious."

In a strange rush of confidence, he almost told Irene to forget the whole case. The urge to return the book to the man and tell him to go back to France was on the tip of his tongue. He'd waited years to get his sisters to visit, and to have their trip cut short because of a case that could have been avoided churned up anger in his stomach.

"That is a good idea," Irene said.

Joe let out a grunt he meant to keep inside.

"What? What is it?"

"Do you not see how angry I am at having to send them home?"

"I do," she said. "It is frustrating that we have to alter our lives because this Frenchman may be dangerous."

"No, Irene. That's not… Well, it is. But it didn't have to be."

"What do you mean? Some cases are dangerous—"

"And some cases didn't need to be taken at all. I wanted to have a nice visit with my sisters, and we could've easily turned down this case. But now, I have to cut my time with my family short to run around and find some gangster's book."

"Cases are important."

"So is family! In fact, I'd say family is more important."

Irene stared straight ahead as she drove.

Joe shifted in the seat to ease the pain in his shoulder from sleeping on the sofa last night. His anger got the better of him and he shouldn't have snapped, but sometimes Irene had blinders on when it came to mysteries.

Even still, he absolutely hated snapping at her.

"Irene—"

"You can visit with your sisters," she said, still staring ahead. "Use the money that Andre gives us, take them out of London and have a proper holiday with them."

"And what will you do? Continue the case?"

"Yes."

"No."

She gave him a glance before looking back at the road.

"You don't want to do this case. And you want to spend time with your sisters because they are important. What am I missing?"

"The fact that you are important to me, too? And I'm not letting you work with this...gangster by yourself."

Her grip tightened on the steering wheel. "I don't understand. You want to visit with your sisters more than solve a case with me, so do so. Solving crimes is my job."

"It is *our* job."

"So, send your sisters home."

Her words were hesitant, and Joe knew she didn't understand. It didn't quell the frustration he felt, though, and the more he tried to gather his thoughts, the more aggravated he became. He should be at the shopping centre with Eleanor and Alice, dragging Irene along despite her half-protests. They should be trying to find a place to buy sweets with him spoiling all three of them. Instead, he was on his way home to tell his sisters to pack up while his best friend weaselled her way into a dangerous man's sight.

"You do this all the time," he snapped. "You pick a case or a course of action without thinking how it will affect other people's lives. Most of the time, it makes no difference and is only a minor inconvenience. But this time, it's a little more complicated. I am trying to handle the outcome as best I can." He pinched his nose, taking a deep breath. "I'm not leaving you, Irene. My sisters will be momentarily mad at me, but you might get hurt or worse. I'm picking the most concerning thing and tending to it."

"I will be alright."

"Dammit, Irene. Please don't make this more convoluted than it already is."

"Fine."

The rest of the ride home was silent, and Joe hated it. He already felt a disconnect from Irene the past few days, and after that conversation about her spending a night with film star Don Radcliffe, it was as if a wall had risen between them. He knew she didn't see it that way, but it felt like he was getting to know his friend all over again. Or perhaps on a different level. Maybe he just cared more about her as the two years had gone on and was now invested in her well-being even more so. Regardless, he didn't know what else to say. He knew his words stung. But they had been true. Of course, he knew Irene's personality and wasn't surprised, but he was a little hurt that her boldness with this case had put all of 221 Baker Street at risk. Would it be different if his sisters weren't here, though? Perhaps, but he didn't want to think of that right now. He wanted to make a point to Irene. He scowled out the front windshield to quell the thoughts playing tennis in his mind.

* * * * *

Neither Alice nor Eleanor were too pleased at having to go home early—until they were given the reason.

"Will he really come after us?" Eleanor said, eyes wide.

"Perhaps," Joe said, waving his hand to encourage them to put their coats on faster.

"I can take him out," Alice muttered. "Me and Irene can."

"No, you can't."

"This is rather exciting," Eleanor paused, boot in hand.

Joe tapped the shoe. "It's not. Hurry on, Lestrade will be here shortly."

As if on cue, the DI appeared at the top of the stairs. There was a twig in his hair and mud smeared on his left knee.

"I thought you had cleared that back garden," he said, slightly breathless.

"It got away from us," Joe clasped his hand.

They all stepped into the flat for a moment while Joe's sisters finished dressing.

"I will take them to Marla's," Lestrade said. "Get them some fish and chip dinner. They can all have a sleepover. Then I'll get them on the first train tomorrow."

"Thank you," Joe breathed. "Truly."

Lestrade looked behind him to Irene, who frantically flipped through the pages of the diary. "Will you both be alright?"

"Yes. I'd just rather not give this Frenchman any excuse to talk to anyone but me or Irene."

"Shall I come back here?"

Irene called over. "No, Eddy. I need you at your office and by your telephone in case I need to ring you about something."

Lestrade looked back at Joe. "Jolly good, then."

They shook hands once more before Joe turned to his sisters. "I'm so sorry your visit was cut short, but I promise you can come back and we will go to all those places and more."

"What about Irene?" Alice asked, tears now welling in her eyes.

He didn't want to speak for Irene and didn't want to make promises she couldn't keep.

Instead, she spoke up herself. "I will be available next time you are here. I will teach you all I know, Alice. And, Eleanor, I will even go shopping and you can curl my hair." Her eyes briefly flicked from the diary to the group at the door, before returning to the pages.

Joe shooed his sisters out the door.

"There you have it. I will ring Marla's later to check on you, and tomorrow before you board the train. Please don't tell mum and dad. Just let them know we took a case."

"Can we tell them about the Frenchman?"

"No, Alice."

"I want to tell them about Scotland Yard."

"Absolutely not, Eleanor. Now go."

Lestrade led them down the stairs and out the back door to the garden. Joe gave his sisters an extra hug, then they traipsed off into the bushes to climb the back fence.

He stood on his tiptoes and could just make out Lestrade's police car in the small alley behind the row of houses. He waited until they took off into the night before returning to the flat.

* * * * *

The living room was empty when he entered, and oddly silent. The clink of a flashing bulb came from the lavatory and he approached cautiously.

"Irene?" He rapped on the door.

Equipment clanged together in the small room before his partner flung open the door, grunting. The camera they'd stolen from Scotland Yard ages ago and the diary they needed to return were bundled in her arms. She dumped the camera on him, then set the book down on the table.

"What were you photographing?"

"Are your sisters away safely?"

Her question over his gave him pause. He thought she'd moved on from them as soon as they were out of the room. Then guilt hit him. He kept thinking as if Irene didn't care about his life, but he had to remember that she was learning to, and he needed to nurture that.

"They are at Marla's. Lestrade is putting them on a train tomorrow. Thank you for asking."

"I was photographing the diary," Irene explained, moving on.

"In the lavatory?" He almost dropped the piece of equipment and understood why. "So the man watching the house would not see the flash."

"Precisely. Now, with them away, are you able to focus?" Irene softened her tone. "I mean… I don't know how to ask it any other way."

He nodded and kept his own voice soft. "I will focus, yes."

"Good. I have telephoned Annette and told her to come through the back garden. You should ring Sarah and tell her to stay away. Then, I will tell you what I know of the author of the diary."

* * * * *

Twenty minutes later, Joe had made his telephone calls and sipped tea in the living room as they waited on Annette. She'd helped them in a previous case and had proved her worth two-fold.

In addition, she spoke French.

Joe had lied to Sarah, stating he was away helping Michael with an animal case. It was cruel and weighed on him, but he knew she wouldn't like the idea of him trapped inside the flat with Irene all day. She wasn't the jealous type, but she had her trepidations about the pair's relationship.

"Do you have your notebook at the ready?"

He stirred his fourth cup of tea of the day and sat at the table, ready to write as she narrated.

"The translations will have to wait, obviously," Irene started. "But the words were written in a few days, as if this diary was the confessions of a dying man. There is cat hair present throughout. I think we can expect more confessions of murder in this book, which is why Mr. Barbier doesn't want us to have it. He is mentioned several times throughout the book. As well as an Amelia and Laverne. There are a few other names that I have written on our board, but none more than those three. I expect one is the wife, and the other a daughter. Or perhaps both daughters."

Joe frowned at his notes. "Not a lot more than what we knew, I'm afraid."

"I am not finished. There is dirt on the corner, dried mud. As if at one point he was writing outside and he dropped the book. There are a few pages spattered with dried blood, but thinned. As if he had sick lungs and coughed up some of them onto the book."

"Confessions of a dying man, indeed."

"Exactly. I believe the cause of death was illness, otherwise he would not have written with such haste. If we could get into Barbier's father's home, then it will tell us more than enough about who would've donated this diary. The translations will tell us if they were donated out of spite or the love toward an old man."

"Perhaps he donated them himself?"

Irene shook her head and opened the diary to near the last page. The writing was barely legible. "The entry is cut short mid-sentence. I have no idea what it says, but there is no end punctuation."

* * * * *

Annette was covered in dirt, with leaves behind each ear, when she arrived at the flat.

"I came as quickly as I could," she panted. "And did exactly as instructed. Over the back wall and through the bushes. I even crawled across the back garden, just in case."

"Possibly unnecessary," Irene said. "But I appreciate the effort."

"Thank you, Miss Holmes. Now, what would you like me to do?"

"First, scrub some dirt off. It's beginning to smell like worms in here and that won't do. Second, we are going to have lunch with a dangerous Frenchman while you stay here and develop photographs of this diary. Then, you will translate each page."

She nodded as her gaze bounced between them. "Is there a reason I cannot have the diary itself to translate?"

"It is going back to the Frenchman, lest he send his men to attempt to murder us all."

"Oh wow," she said, stepping out to the hall to brush some dirt off her. "What a case to step in to!"

"Indeed." Irene turned to Joe. "I am using the lavatory, then we are leaving."

Once she left, Annette turned to him as well. "Thank you again for ringing me! This sounds most exciting!"

"It's most dangerous. Did Irene not warn you?"

"Yes. Well, sort of. She told me I was not to be seen and sneak in the back garden."

Joe nodded. "Just stay on this side of the light. There is a man watching the flat. He will see us leave, and he needs to think the place empty. Understand?"

"Yes, Doctor Watson. I completely understand. I will use the lavatory to develop the pictures."

"Also," Joe said, surprised he was only thinking of this now. "Ring the museum. See if they remember who donated this diary. Push for any answer you can find."

Irene reappeared and headed to the hall. "Come Joe. Let's get this lunch over with. Annette, stay safe and get that diary translated. Oh, but first, listen to Doctor Watson and ring the museum."

With a proud smile on his face, he followed his partner out the door.

Chapter V

Into the Thick of the Mystery

The hotel restaurant was far busier for lunch, but that didn't stop Mr. Andre Barbier from renting a private booth near the back again. Despite Joe and his attitude, Irene instructed him to tell the Frenchman nothing, as if they hadn't seen anything of the diary. It would be tricky to keep the information from Andre as he most definitely knew more than he let on, but they'd try, nonetheless.

He leaned back in his chair as they approached, blue-green eyes fixed on Irene. Barbier was a good-looking man, even beautiful—but the kind of beauty found in predators.

Irene would not be prey today.

When they reached the table, the two men on either side of the Frenchman pulled out the chairs for Irene and Joe. Andre held his palm out, requesting the diary. She dug the book from her bag and placed it on the table under his hand, and settled back in the seat.

A wicked glint flashed in his eyes, and she felt Joe tense even more beside her.

"Where is the second book?"

Irene had to admit, his accent, though cutting, was rather pleasing as far as foreign accents went.

"There was no second book. We only acquired one."

"There were two taken from my father's estate." Andre was looking between them both as if one of them would magically pull the book from either of their bags.

"We do not have it," Irene stated again. "Whomever took this one must have kept it."

"Or the man who delivered that book to you still has it."

"He does not, I am certain. Now, we will take our fee and begin our questions to solve this case promptly."

"You will add finding the second book to the case." He glanced around again, as if one of his men had suddenly found it under a table. "I would expect whoever took the books still has the second one. You should find it when you find them."

"'Should' does not always equal 'will'."

"I have faith in you, though." Andre smirked. He snapped his fingers in the air and the man to his right reached into his coat, passing an envelope to his boss. "Here you go, Mrs. Holmes"

Irene took it and in turn and passed it to Joe to count. As she opened her mouth to begin her questioning, a young woman came by with a tray full of hearty sandwiches and different hors d'oeuvres.

"Please eat." Andre gestured to the food.

Irene drooled as she looked over the platters, debating if taking a sandwich would be playing into this man's game.

However, when he reached out for one, she followed suit. Joe, on the other hand, remained stoic, keeping his eyes on the Frenchman.

Irene took a smaller bite of the sandwich than she normally would, as she wanted her questions to be clear and concise.

"Do you know the motivation behind donating your father's belongings to the museum?"

He chuckled, like the answer was obvious. "To seek revenge on me? To anger me?"

"You think it has nothing to do with your father, then?"

He paused. "I am not sure."

Joe still denied himself a sandwich, but scribbled diligently in his notebook. Irene wasn't too concerned with his lack of eating, though neither one of them turned down food often.

"Where were the diaries kept?" she continued. "I imagine somewhere in London, unless the culprit brought it all the way from France."

"My father's estate, outside of the city."

"Who do you believe donated these items?"

Darkness swept across the man's brow as he finished his food. "There are only three people who dared touch my father's belongings other than me: my mother, my father's mistress, and my uncle, who is long dead."

"Your father had a mistress?" Joe finally asked a question, not looking up from his notes.

"Of course. Everybody knew about Laverne, including my mother."

Having finished her sandwich, Irene ran her tongue along her teeth. The way Andre spoke about Laverne, even for that short amount of time—with an up tilt in his voice—told her that he was fond of this woman. "Was your mother upset about her husband seeing someone else?"

He shrugged and detached immediately from the conversation. "She did not seem to care, and if she did, I never heard her talk about it. We lived in France until the war, when I went off to fight. When I came home, they were in London for good. I stayed in France, with all of our friends, other family and business partners."

"How, then, did you know your father's belongings were even missing?"

Mr. Barbier had been truthful so far, though he was good at omitting things.

"After he passed, I came to the estate to collect what I could."

"He died from an illness," Irene noted. "It took him quickly once it set in."

For the first time since the meeting, the Frenchman faltered. He hesitated, and his eyes narrowed briefly before he answered.

"Yes, it did. My mother and Laverne had already taken so many things by the time I got there, but his personal diaries were of no importance to anyone but him. And they were not at his bedside table, where he usually kept them."

"Where were your mother and Laverne? Were neither one of them there?"

"No."

"Then how did you know the items were donated and not simply stolen and recovered by the museum?"

"There was a letter at the house thanking us for our donation."

Thoughts flew through Irene's mind. She felt like she held an egg with the smallest of cracks and there was so much more inside to see. She needed to explore this estate, talk to both the wife and mistress, dig her fingers into this mystery.

"Where is the estate—"

"No. You will not go there."

"Why not?" Irene snapped, ready for the unexpected fight.

"It's the source of the missing items."

"I will not have police at my father's house."

"We're not police."

"But you are partners with them. No police."

To everyone's surprised, Joe snorted out a laugh.

"Something funny?" Andre asked.

Joe shook his head. "You are becoming hostile and we are simply trying to do the job you asked of us."

Irene stared at her friend for a moment, unable to hide her surprise. Joe's brow was furrowed; he was gripping his pen like a weapon. She had no idea what had him riled up, but she needed to press on with her questions.

"Where are your mother and Laverne?"

"Laverne used to own a seamstress shop in the city. I have no idea where my mother is."

"Where is this shop?"

"I do not know."

"Can I have the letter from the museum?"

"I threw it into the fire."

"I need to go to your father's estate." Irene tried again, keeping her voice stern.

"My mother's name is Amelia Barbier. You can find her using that, can't you? And you will not step foot in the estate."

Swallowing her frustration like stale bread, Irene leaned forward. "I can find the address on my own. Hell, the museum must have it since they sent a letter."

She expected Joe's knee to bump hers under the table as a reminder to keep calm, but it never came. All she felt was his annoyance.

Andre shook his head. "It was unaddressed, given to the person who donated the items when they dropped them at the desk. Also, if you try to go to the estate, you will not be welcomed."

Irene sighed purposefully and stood.

"You have given me nothing. A woman who runs a seamstress shop. That's it. You will not even let me near the source of the case. How am I to do my job without information?"

The Frenchman remained seated. "Because that is what you do, or so I have heard. Act like you are the best and solve this."

She could practically feel Joe vibrating beside her.

Had they done more with less? Of course. But this man assumed too much and was threatening, thinking he had the upper hand. And Irene wanted to wipe the smug smile off his face.

Joe stood. "Perhaps we should go. You have your diary back. We should end this here."

Irene fought the urge to look at her partner in surprise. It was unlike him to cut a conversation short, unless she was ready to take a swing at the person on the other side. But she'd done a decent job of keeping herself calm, and if anything, it was Joe who looked ready to swing.

He put his hand on her shoulder and shuffling feet came from behind them. Joe tightened his grip and moved behind her, putting his chest at her back in a protective stance.

She stared down at Andre. After almost a minute, the Frenchman raised his hand to the third man behind him, who produced an envelope. Andre tossed it across the table to Irene.

In it were two photographs, and the rest of their money.

"My mother has the dark hair and Laverne has the mark on her cheek. I have provided what information I have to give, and more than enough for you to use. You will finish this case. You will not involve the police. And when everything is over, I will return to France with my missing items and the person responsible in my hands."

Irene handed the envelope to Joe. "Neither one of us speaks French. It would be beneficial to have a translator."

"Anything you find, you can report immediately to me."

"Shall I ring you in the middle of the night if I find one sentence that needs translating? I certainly can, but you may not like being woken at three in the morning by my voice. That brings up another point. How are we to contact you? This whole charade does not lend itself to hiring an investigator. You will have to drop some of your bravado if you want this solved."

A muscle in his jaw twitched. "You may telephone the hotel and ask for me."

She should've walked away, but the crack she saw urged her to pry it open.

She tapped the table with her fingertip. Joe responded by squeezing her shoulders, warning her not to pry.

"Although we have had more interesting mysteries and certainly more cooperative clients, we shall work you into our schedule because this has intrigued me."

That muscle in Mr. Barbier's jaw twitched again. He pointed at the three men with him. "Do you see them, Mrs. Holmes? They will ensure the case is solved."

"If you're trying to scare us, it won't work," Joe voiced her thoughts.

Andre narrowed his eyes at Joe, but Irene shifted her weight to capture his attention. "He's right. This is my city, and nothing scares me. Not even your gorillas."

The man smiled, full and big, showing off gleaming white teeth. "Let's hope I don't have to prove you wrong, then. Good luck, Mrs. Holmes."

With the conversation done, Joe kept hold of her as he muscled his way through the two men standing behind them. Though slight, Joe was tall and broad-shouldered. He managed to knock one of the men askew as he went.

Irene followed him through the restaurant, never taking her eyes off him. He set his shoulders, ready to fight anyone who dared jump in his way. He even ignored the hotel staff, as she wished them a good day.

"You're troubled." Irene said as they exited the building.

"I am," he replied, holding the door for her. "I hate bullies."

She snorted. "We've dealt with our fair share, Joe."

"I know, but these men… Him… I don't know. It irked me in particular this time. Maybe I am just on edge and feeling protective. I am also tired because, though I love napping on the sofa, it is not good for multiple nights."

"Take my bed until Miss Hudson can fix up your room again after your sisters. I can sleep anywhere."

He sighed. "No. It's fine. I don't like being forced to do something I don't want to. Especially something dangerous."

Irene was going to remark that they always dealt with dangerous people, but she bit her tongue. Joe's worry went much deeper than the Frenchman and his troops. He'd been captured during the war and forced to traipse around doing the German soldiers' bidding until he was freed. He used to have panic-induced episodes, but it had been almost a year since Irene could recall him having one. Regardless, Joe was already mad, and this lunch fed into his anger.

As they drove home, guilt wormed its way into her. His words had not left her head. His frustration toward her and this case was burned into her mind. Joe had been mad at her only twice before.

She should have offered her bed when she first found out he was sleeping on the sofa. Joe's tall body didn't fit many places at the best of times, let alone on the sofa. Being much smaller, she could easily sleep in the living area, or anywhere for that matter.

More guilt ate away at her as she parked the automobile in front of 221. She followed Joe in, but stopped in the foyer.

"Joe?"

He paused and looked back at her.

"I am sorry," she said, looking straight up at him. "I think I understand why you are mad. I truly did not mean to put your sisters in harm's way and I should have foreseen how a case like this would do so. I get excited about cases, because that is all I have. You have a whole life. Relationships with others, a family, another career to step into at any moment. I do not. I have Baker Street and my mysteries, and sometimes I worry that they will go away, and when they go away, so will you. I know that is not true, but I do worry sometimes and I cannot help it. And that worry turns to eagerness at the cost of others."

"Irene..." His voice was soft as he shuffled closer to her, but she kept going.

"Last winter was long and awful and I am worried that this one will be the same and that you will be gone for a lot of it because you want to go to the vet practice, or with Sarah. You could go away with her on holiday and I couldn't stop you because then I would be a bad friend. Also, I need to solve cases, because if I don't..." She ran out of breath and sucked in another as Joe moved even closer. "I apologize again. I did not mean to blurt all that out to you, especially on a case—"

He grabbed her and pulled her to him, wrapping her in a tight hug. Her arms were trapped at her side, face pressed into his shoulder, cheek squished into the fabric of his coat. She let him hug her for a full minute before he finally released her. He kept hold of her shoulders, though, forcing her to listen to him.

"Never apologize for sharing your feelings with me, Irene." he said, all traces of anger and annoyance gone. "My sisters are safe, I have no plans to return to the vet practice full-time, and I promise you with my whole heart that I am not leaving Baker Street any time soon. Okay?"

The guilt in her stomach was replaced with another slithery feeling—one that wasn't wholly negative—as she stared up at Joe. His eyes were tired, his hair needed a shampoo, but he was earnest.

"Also, perhaps my words were a bit harsh—"

"They were not. They were true."

"Regardless, I commend you for recognizing why I was upset." He turned to the stairs, keeping an arm around her shoulder. "The woman I met a year and a half ago would've never even come close to seeing any sort of emotion in others, nor would she acknowledge it."

She snorted. "Then I am becoming soft."

"No, you're a friend who cares about the people she loves."

"Exactly," she said, exceptionally glad the conversation had turned light. "Soft."

"Soft is good sometimes," he said as they climbed the stairs.

Irene wanted to mumble back an argument, but left it alone. Joe was not mad at her anymore and would hopefully be back to his normal self—which was needed, because she had a feeling this case was about to get trickier.

When they entered the flat, Annette looked up at them with big, excited eyes.

"Things are going quite well," she said. "I have stayed back from the windows, and on this side of the lights so they don't see any shadows. I've developed the photographs and have translated a good bit of the diary. It is a funny dialect, and some words are smudged, but I'll show you what I have. I also have not rung the museum yet, as I was so engrossed in these words, but I can ring them at once."

Joe set the envelope from Barbier on the table and sank into a chair. Irene remained standing, glancing at all the translated pages.

"Tell us what you have for now."

"There is almost every crime mentioned that I can think of. Money transferring hands, more locations of where people may be buried."

"Andre, the son. How many times is he mentioned?"

"Many. But it doesn't appear he had much to do with the crimes. He went to fight before he could really help with anything, and it's mentioned that he had no interest in any of the goings on with the family. When he returned, it's written that he was like a different person. His father mentions the words 'broken' and 'scared'. He tried to help, but the business was in shambles. From what I could piece together, this Andre wanted to dress nice and spend money. After the family fled France, they fell out of touch, but he hopes that his son doesn't follow in his footsteps. He sounds like a very guilty and sad man."

"What about mention of Amelia or Laverne?"

Annette nodded. "They are both in here, though he speaks about them more later on. It's as if he wanted to confess his crimes before talking about his personal life. Laverne's last name is Dubois, if that is of any help."

Irene paced from the kitchen to the living area and back again. She was determined to find the estate, as that would tell her so much more. However, she didn't want to waste time or risk a fight with Andre.

While these translations were decent, and told them about Andre's father, their goal was finding the wife and mistress. Only, their single lead was a seamstress shop. Easy to search out, but again, time consuming. There had to be more information in the rest of the diary, which meant they had to wait for Annette to translate more.

"Keep going," she instructed the girl.

"What shall we do?" Joe asked from his chair. "I suppose the only thing is to visit the museum and see if they know who donated the diary. Renaux said it was anonymous, but a note of thanks was passed along to a person."

Irene nodded. "That's precisely what we shall do. Annette, same rules as before. Should you need anything, carefully descend the stairs and speak to Miss Hudson quietly."

"Understood, Miss Holmes."

Joe stood from the chair as Irene grabbed her jacket.

"On our way out, we will consult with Miss Hudson and see if she has been to a seamstress who speaks French, or knows of one, and perhaps we will visit a few."

As the pair pulled on their boots, a loud thump came from the front door. Miss Hudson mumbled as she opened the door, then she shrieked, shrill and loud.

Irene hurried downstairs, Joe at her heels. The landlady stood frozen in the foyer.

A skinny man lay on the front pavement, curled in the fetal position. At the stirring, he unfolded his body and looked up at them. Half his face was swollen, black and blue, and his wrists had rope marks where he'd been bound.

"Miss…Holmes? Help…" Hubert Renaux's shaky voice pleaded.

"Get him inside," Irene ordered.

As Joe and Miss Hudson dragged the poor man indoors, she stepped out into the street. Drops of blood on the pavement, and tire marks bumping the curbs. The tracks belonged to a large automobile, not unlike the one that sat halfway down the street. She made a point of staring at the driver, too far away to see properly.

The auto didn't move for a solid ten seconds, then the engine started, pulling away from the curb. She watched the car drive around the corner before turning back toward the house.

Chapter VI

Translating a French Diary

Annette and Miss Hudson worked to clean up the translator as he sat shaking on the dining chair. At the same time, Irene paced, waiting to speak to him, and Joe simply stared at the man. The beating had been brutal, but all that he could think about was that this man told Barbier where they lived. And because he did so, they were all in danger. He didn't want to be angry. He wanted to empathize, as he knew what it was like being hurt for information. However, he was tired and worried about his sisters'—and his and Irene's—safety. They needed this man, of course. Annette was good at translating, but he would be much faster. Plus, the girl could help search for other things that came to light while Joe and Irene ran around the city. Yet, those thoughts didn't quell his trepidation.

Having Renaux sitting in their flat, beaten and bruised, was clearly a message from Barbier. A helping hand, yes, but also a warning. The sooner he left, the better.

Annette stepped away from him with the last of the bandages. No sooner had Renaux taken a breath than Joe slapped the photographs of the diary in front of him.

"Translate these. Now."

Renaux shrunk back. As Joe opened his mouth to order the man again, Irene grabbed his arm.

She dragged him, quite forcefully, toward her bedroom.

"You are angry again," she said. "I thought we solved that. Also, you are bleeding."

She flipped his left hand over, exposing his palm. Four nail marks indented into the skin, one of them oozing out a drop of red liquid. Joe wiped his palm on his trousers and flexed his fingers, attempting to relax.

"He gave our address to Barbier."

Irene nodded. "He did. However, we need him. You must keep your head."

"Why do I feel like this conversation should be the opposite?"

"Because normally you are the one talking sense into me. I am allowed to be emotional and angry. You, however, are the one who must keep calm and ensure I do not to anything irrational. Those are our roles."

Joe chuckled, exhaustion hitting him. "But what happens if I do not want to be calm? What if I want to be angry?"

She straightened his collar and fixed his uneven sleeves. "Then you can be so after the case. Mr. Renaux will not be here for long. We get him to translate the rest of the diary quickly, then we send him away with some train ticket money. Out the back door, through the garden. I don't want him here, but if he gets captured again, and Barbier finds out we have copies of the diary, we will be in even more danger. Also, seeing you this riled up makes me uncomfortable."

"I wish we could let him go, but I understand why we can't."

Irene nodded, frowning. For a moment, Joe thought she might offer a hug. While not completely out of the ordinary, she usually reserved those for excited moments and bursts of happiness.

No hug came, instead, she grasped both his hands and looked at him.

"What are you doing?"

"Calming you down," she said, as if he asked the most ridiculous question. "Whenever you have one of your episodes, you grab onto me."

"I am not having an episode."

"But you are riled. So, this will help. Is it working?"

She seemed genuinely concerned, and though the act of holding her hands pulled him from a panic-induced episode, this was wholly different. He was also resisting calming down. He wanted to be a little mad, despite all Irene had done to apologize and to help him calm down. He wanted to be frustrated at the world for ruining his weekend with his family and for handing them such a dangerous case.

His best friend was trying to help, though. Trying to ease him back to his normal self in the only way he'd shown her how.

As he stared into Irene's big brown eyes, a part of the anger did crumble away. She didn't blink, but her expression was soft and earnest. A rarity. Usually she wore a mask, a persona for the rest of the world. Annoyed, unimpressed, disappointed. Furrowed brows, a scowl. But now Irene looked up at him as she tried her best to keep him calm. Her lipstick was faded, she still had a smudge of dirt on her jawbone, and the bags under her eyes were darker than normal.

She looked beautiful.

That thought threatened to branch out, which thrummed up his heart all over again. For a brief, fleeting moment, he wondered what she thought— similar or not—when she looked at him.

Joe cleared his throat and tried to keep his voice strong to not betray his wandering mind. "It's helping a lot."

"Grand!" Irene dropped his hands and, within less than a second, she was back to being pragmatic. "Let's move on. We have places to be."

He sighed, suddenly feeling silly for entertaining the idea that she thought about anything other than solving the case. Shaking his head, he followed her out of the bedroom and back to reality.

Miss Hudson had brought tea and returned downstairs. Annette stood behind the translator.

"I told him we needed information on the wife and mistress."

"I do not like this, Miss Holmes," Renaux stammered. "They kept asking me about a second book. What second book? I was given only the one!"

"We know," Irene said. "And we do not care about your feelings toward the situation. You brought this to our doorstep and now you must help. Translate everything you can, as quickly as you can, then you will sneak out the back garden, get on a train and leave London for a few days until this case is done. Now, read."

The man hesitated but Irene's stern look spurred him into action.

* * * * *

Half an hour later, Joe had two pages' worth of notes from the translations. There were more confessions of murders from before the first war, alongside stories of thievery, extortion, and prostitution.

There were also confessions of love. Not many, as this diary seemed to mostly relate to crimes. However, this man adored Laverne, the mistress, so much that he had bought her a flat in London, and all the jewellery she could want.

He also seemed to love his wife, Amelia, though he mentioned her foul temper and almost cruel nature. And yet, they stayed married until his death.

Renaux started into a paragraph describing the new flat that Mr. Barbier had purchased for Laverne. It was in the north of London and he picked that building specifically so she could see the red spire of the church she attended.

The moment the translator spoke that line, Irene slammed her hand on the table. "Red spire? That is what it says? Are you certain?"

"Yes. Very certain. It is mentioned twice."

"Does it say which way the flat faces?" Joe joined in.

"No. Just that she can see the red spire when she sits by the fireplace."

Irene pivoted and paced around the room. Joe scribbled that note in his book and circled it. Not one church came to his mind, though, as the last time he'd been to mass was with his parents as a young man before going to veterinary college.

"Miss Holmes?" Renaux's words were weak, his voice exhausted. "I want to go home now. There is nothing more in this diary which we don't already know, or that Miss Annette hasn't already translated."

Irene spun to him. "You are only saying that so you can leave."

He shook his head as Annette turned the book toward her.

"He's correct, Miss Holmes," she confirmed, flipping through the last few pages. "There is nothing more, from what I can tell. The writing is very hard to read and the words become erratic."

"As if he's dying."

Both Annette and Renaux nodded.

Irene looked to Joe for some answer he didn't have. If that was all the diary said, then they didn't need this man anymore. The sleuth looked eager to hunt for this red spire, and Joe couldn't blame her. It was the first lead they had—other than a few more places where bodies were long buried—and those skeletons wouldn't tell them much.

"Sneak out the back," Irene said to Renaux.

"The back, miss?"

She nodded. "I don't want the man out there to capture you again, lest you tell him what we know *again*. Go out the back and to the left. All the way around the block and hail a cab."

When he didn't move right away, Irene shooed him with a flick of her wrist.

"Come, I'll show you," Annette offered, leading him out the door.

Once they were down the stairs, Irene spun to Joe. "First, we must utilize that girl more. Did you see that? She took him away, and I didn't even have to get mean."

Joe chuckled. "I always forget that you are aware most times when you are blunt with someone."

"Of course I know. I am careful of every word that comes out of my mouth... Mostly. Anyway, we must ask Miss Hudson if she knows any churches with a red spire, as neither of us are church-going individuals."

"Maybe that's our problem," Joe mused to himself.

"I see no problem with us," Irene huffed. "What would religion add? A false sense of hope? A belief that I am not in command of my own life?"

Joe held up his hands in defeat. He knew Irene didn't have a religious bone in her body, but they'd never really discussed it. And now was not the time for such a discussion.

They both grabbed their jackets as Annette hurried back up. "He's away."

"Splendid," Irene said. "Stay here. We will ring you if we need anything more. Otherwise, we shall return with successful news."

The pair hurried down the stairs and ran into their landlady waiting by the door, peering out the side window.

"Miss Hudson," Joe took her arm gently. "Everything is fine, but please step away from the window."

He doubted Barbier would want to hurt an old woman, but the risk wasn't worth it. The last thing he needed was Miss Hudson injured and Irene out for blood.

Mostly because he wouldn't stop her, and would be at her heels.

"Do you know of any churches with red spires?" He asked once she was safely in the foyer.

"That survived the war," Irene added.

The older woman thought, tilting her head back and forth. "Hm, not really. The only one I can think of is the one over on St. John's, I believe. Big red spire, can't miss it."

Irene glanced at Joe, but kept her mouth shut, refraining from saying the something sarcastic.

"Thank you," she said instead, then pivoted away again, leaving Joe to chase after her.

Irene made it over the back fence first. As Joe landed beside her with a grunt, she sighed.

"You know what this proves? That we sorely need an office."

He picked a twig from her dark curls. "I couldn't agree more. We do have to go somewhere, though. Barbier is not going to believe we stayed in Baker Street all day."

"We will go to the library later. And we shall take a taxi and bill Mr. Barbier for it. But for now, we will sneak as much as possible."

The pair fetched a taxi and had it drop them down the road from the church. They both took a quick look around the street, but Joe didn't see any of the large black cars that Barbier's men drove, nor did he see anyone skulking about watching them.

Irene must've deemed the coast clear as well, because she started down the street. They'd made it halfway when the church came into view.

"There is the red spire," Joe pointed.

Irene stopped so abruptly that he bumped into her. There was only one apartment building in which you could see the spire from.

Automobiles stopped at the curb, parking or dropping tenants off. It reminded Joe of the flats they were in when they investigated the case with the Irish Setters: full of marble, shiny appliances and lifts that reached the top floor faster than any car.

And a diligent doorman assuring no strangers entered the building, especially investigators looking for the mistress of a French gangster.

As Joe opened his mouth to discuss their options, Irene grabbed his arm. She jerked him into the small space between the building and its neighbour.

"We are returning from an early dinner," she said, dark eyes big and wild.

"What?"

"We belong—"

"Oh, no, Irene," Joe cut her off, figuring out her plan. "We've snuck into places before, but have never pretended to be other people so boldly. If he's any doorman worth his salt, he will know we don't belong."

"We will do our best to get past him, go straight to the administration office and find out where Laverne lives before he catches on. Let's go."

Before Joe could protest again, she hooked her arm in his and tugged him back to the pavement, then changed her walk completely. She swayed her hips and laughed the most high-pitched giggle Joe had heard. Normally, a girly laugh was a pleasant sound, but it was so odd coming from Irene; it made him uneasy.

However, the boldness with which she marched them up to the building gave him a bit of confidence. He straightened himself and set his shoulders.

They approached the doorman, and Irene gave a curt nod. "Alfred. Pleasant evening out."

"It is," he said automatically and opened the door for them.

Irene tensed her grip on Joe as they both sped up a step, heading through the lobby and down the hallway. She released him as they found the small hallway with a few offices.

"Keep a lookout," she commanded, then scrambled into the administration office.

Joe had no idea where the building manager was, or if he was set to return anytime soon, but he stood at attention in the hall and listened. At the same time, he heard Irene rummaging through the room behind him. She banged her arms or some appendage multiple times in her hurry, cussing under her breath.

All was quiet so far in the hallway, which made all hairs on his arms stand on edge. He expected someone to pop out at any moment and arrest them. He was sure they didn't have enough clout to talk their way out of an arrest. And he would hate to put Lestrade in an awkward position.

Heavy shoes echoed from far down the hall and a deep grumbling followed. Alfred was on to them.

"We have to go, Irene," Joe urged.

After a few more colourful cuss words, Irene exclaimed, "Ah ha! Found her!"

They scrambled from the room as Alfred came around the corner. "You two! Stop!"

Joe led the way around the corner to the long hallway toward the rear entrance. As they passed the back door, he flung it open, but carried on to the stairs. Hopefully, Irene had the same idea and followed him. Luckily, he felt her at his back soon enough.

They paused at the first floor, catching their breath.

Irene leaned on him. "That was excellent thinking. Well done."

Alfred's steps were gloriously not present on the stairs.

"What floor is Laverne on?"

Irene glanced at the paper. "Eighth."

They both looked up and sighed in unison.

"There is a lift," Joe offered.

Neither of them were fond of the machine, but time was not on their side, and today had been long enough without climbing seven floors.

"Fine," Irene said, as if being forced to endure something horrific. "But I refuse to let go of your hand until we are at our floor."

Joe's lips tugged upward as he followed his friend to the first-floor hallway to the lift. For all the bravery she had, the small travelling box unnerved her every time.

They stepped in and Irene immediately squeezed his hand, brow furrowed, as if daring the lift to scare her. The box started up and Joe felt his stomach bottom out a bit. He didn't like the lift either, but he always put on a brave face for Irene, even if she didn't notice. The ride was a long one, but they eventually made it. Laverne's flat was the second from the end.

Irene gave a sharp knock on the door once they'd arrived.

A petite lady with a slim face and deep lines opened the door. She had the sharp eyes of someone who didn't miss a thing.

"Yes?"

"Laverne DuBois? I am Irene Holmes and this is my partner, Doctor Watson. We have some questions for you pertaining to a Francois Barbier."

Joe already had a business card out to hand her. The lady studied it carefully, then turned her sharp gaze back to them.

"How did you get into the building?" Her French accent was slightly softer than Barbier's.

"Alfred let us in," Irene said.

"Oh, okay." She stepped back and unlocked the chain.

The foyer was stunning in bright marbles and golds. The interior of the flat was even more impressive, and almost too big for a single woman.

No cup of tea was offered; Joe found that odd. Perhaps it was French culture, or perhaps this lady was too nervous?

She led them to a luxurious sitting room filled with plush reds and golds.

"Have you come on behalf of Andre?" she asked immediately. Though her accent was thick, her sentences were easy to understand and her flow of words was that of someone who'd spoken English for a long time.

"Not particularly," Irene answered. "A book belonging to Francois was donated to the museum, and we are attempting to find out who donated it."

"And you will bring the results of your findings back to Andre." The woman smiled. "Don't look surprised, Miss Holmes. If this were a fiction novel with his name in it, there would be no reason for a private detective to be looking for it. What book was this of Francois'?"

"A personal diary," Joe offered. "We are wondering who would even want to send this piece of personal history to somewhere so public."

"After Francois died, did you return to the estate?" Irene jumped in.

"I did. If only to collect anything I may have found interesting, but there was nothing. His wife, Amelia, was there when I visited. She had picked the house clean by the time I got there, determined to take everything she could sell. She told me she didn't want anything more and that I could burn the place for all she cared, so I told her I would."

Barbier had been cryptic about why they couldn't go back, and simply said the place was 'inaccessible'. Though, if it was burned down, that would've been a simple enough answer.

"We know Amelia knew of you." Joe jumped in on the questioning. "It didn't seem to bother her? She didn't attempt to confront you at all?"

"No. She found out quite quickly. They fought often, and he tried to use me as a threat, but she really didn't care."

"Why? She was his wife."

"It was an arranged marriage between them," Laverne explained, adjusting the hem of her dress. "He had a lot of money and kept their marriage alive by giving her a hefty allowance every week. He did the same with me, though his doting on me was a bit more personal. She never cared for him or Andre. She was a horrible mother to him. Used to hit him and lock him up."

Joe glanced at Irene, but all she did was study the woman.

"That is not mentioned in the diary."

Her sharp eyes flicked to him. "You have the diary? You've read it?"

"We have, yes," Irene finally interjected. "There are a lot of crimes in there. But they are old, most not even worth going to Scotland Yard for."

Laverne stared at Irene, as if processing her words. She pursed her lips together and fixed her hem again.

Joe tried his very best to read the woman's body language, but she kept so still and tight-lipped that he scratched half of his notes out.

She seemed disappointed about something, though.

"I offered to take Andre as my own son a number of times," Laverne said. "But Amelia became possessive of him, as if me taking him would anger Francois and cut her off from her money. Everyone but her was heartbroken when he went off to war. Well, Andre wasn't heartbroken. He was eager to leave and even lied about his age to go fight. He mentioned wanting to live with me several times, but she wouldn't let him, and his father insisted he learn the family business." Laverne signed. "I want to reach out to him, but I am worried he will be too far gone or he will not want to see me. If he sent you, can you please get me in contact with him?"

Joe kept his mouth shut. They had no idea how Barbier felt about Laverne and he didn't want to anger the Frenchman because they gave away information they weren't supposed to.

Irene answered, however, short and abrupt, with the kind of urgency that told Joe she had a thought and wanted to run with it.

"We cannot. Regarding Francois, we've heard he was a once-in-a-generation man, and he has a great legacy to leave."

The lady's eye twitched, as if she hated every word that Irene spoke. Joe hastily wrote in his book. This woman seemed to have loved Francois, but there was something he couldn't place. Of course, the apathy could be the years from the war, the sudden move to London, or the fact that she thought she probably didn't need to speak about him or his family ever again.

"He did a lot of things," she finally said. "Many of them are not great. I would assume there were some tales in that diary that would get him into quite a bit of trouble if he were still alive."

Irene shrugged. "Nothing from this decade, and mostly in France."

Irene was lying. She'd picked up on something Joe had missed and he was eager to end the conversation and figure out what that something was.

"Only a few more questions," Irene said. "Before you burned the house down, you wouldn't have donated some of his belongings to the museum? Not even to preserve your place in the history of the family?"

She let out a lovely laugh, breaking her seemingly nervous streak. "I worked in aid stations through the past two wars. I have greater stories to tell than collecting money and the occasional night with an old Frenchman."

"Do you know where Amelia is?"

Laverne shrugged. "Last I heard, she opened a restaurant. Or she wanted to. After Francois died, we parted ways. I would be surprised if she was still in the city. She hated London."

Irene stood. "Thank you for your time."

Chapter VII

A Waste of a Case

Irene hurried out of the flat, mind racing.

"I dislike her. She seemed both disappointed that we had dismissed the diary and its contents, and yet eager to find out more information."

"You were overplaying its dullness," Joe said, huffing to keep up with her as they descended the stairs.

"Why would Barbier not mention the estate burned down? Would he assume we wouldn't even try to work the case?"

Joe's knees worked overtime as they reached the third floor. "Perhaps she didn't do a good enough job, and he burned the rest. Or maybe he burned the rest with some people in there."

They finally reached the first floor. They exited out the back door and paused.

"Now what?" he asked.

Irene paced on the pavement, contemplating Laverne's words.

"We search for French restaurants in London and visit them."

"You truly think Amelia opened a restaurant here?"

She nodded. "If Barbier hated her so much, she probably wouldn't be allowed to open a restaurant anywhere in France. But if she stayed here, she'd be able to because he clearly doesn't like this city. Also, Francois loved London and probably left her pounds instead of whatever they use in France."

"Francs."

"Sure. Come, we have to find a directory of the French restaurants in London."

* * * * *

"Perhaps we can actually eat at one of these restaurants?" Joe suggested as they visited their fourth. They had six in total and the first three did not have a manager or employee named Amelia Barbier. Their next stop was a small storefront, but the rooms went far to the back. Bread accosted Irene's nose immediately. Perhaps they *would* stay for something to eat even if Amelia wasn't here.

A young woman came to them with a smile on her face. "We are looking for Amelia," Irene said. "We're old friends of hers and heard she opened this place."

Before, this had been met with raised brows and shakes of heads. This young woman's eyes, however, lit up, and she nodded.

"She is just in her office. I shall retrieve her."

She scurried away to the back of the restaurant and, within a minute, hurried back, Amelia following.

"Who are you?" the woman snapped. She was slim but had strong arms under rolled up sleeves.

Irene couldn't quite place why, but she looked mean. Like a small dog who'd nip at anyone that passed.

"I am Irene Holmes. And this is my partner, Doctor Watson. We are here investigating the donation of your husband's belongings."

She waved them off with bony, roughened hands. "He is dead."

"We know," Joe said. "And his diary was donated to a museum."

This caught her attention. She motioned for them to follow her.

As they weaved through the tables, Irene's stomach growled. She had no idea what French cuisine even was, but it smelled wonderfully sweet and hearty.

Amelia led them into a small office full of papers.

"What was in the diary? Who asked you to find me? What do you know about Francois?"

Joe stepped back at her barrage of questions, but Irene stood her ground. This woman's accent made her questions harsh, but they were all normal.

"Not much at all. There were simply confessions of old crimes. Your son wants to know who donated it to the museum, however. It did not say much about you, just that you did not like either him or your son."

The woman snorted at the insult. "Andre was a terrible boy. And I was only with Francois because our family decreed it. This was no secret to anyone, though. Do any of these crimes involve me? If they do, then it is a lie. I did nothing like that with Francois. I was just there to—"

"Spend his money," Irene interrupted. "We know. Did you leave the estate immediately after he died?"

She nodded. "Why would I stay? I took what I wanted and left. The girl…Laverne…showed up. Have you spoken to her? She said she would burn everything to the ground because she was so heartbroken. Puh, I said to her go ahead. I have no love for anything here."

"And you haven't been back since?"

She raised a sharp eyebrow. "Why would I go back? I have everything and it is burned to the ground."

Irene nodded in agreement, but glanced at Joe. She had suspicions but couldn't quite place them.

"Were you there when Laverne burned the estate?"

Amelia shook her head. "No. She said she would do it, though I have no idea what she would gain. She had nothing there, and it was not as if she was angry at my family. She had everything she wanted and didn't even have to live with Francois or Andre."

"What is the address of the estate?"

"Did Andre not tell you? He was always an odd boy. So possessive of his home, though he was never happy there. I will write it down for you. I have nothing to hide. The crimes were all Francois. Until Andre started to help him; then only God knows what he did."

She wrote the address down on a notepad from her desk and handed it to Joe. "You think there are still things there to collect?"

"If it is all burned, then probably not," Joe said.

"True, but perhaps I should go back to look."

Irene shook her head. "I think its best if you stay away, for your own safety."

The last thing they needed was Mrs. Barbier showing up and destroying any evidence that might still be at the house—or finding anything that might be important to this case.

"That will be all," Irene said. "Though we will take two of your most French dishes."

"We have fresh quiche Lorraine. You may take one so long as you return if you find anything interesting in that estate."

* * * * *

"What is quiche Lorraine?" Joe asked, staring at the wrapped round dish in his lap. "It smells of an omelette but in a pie."

"Not a clue," Irene said as they sat in the back of the cab on the way to Baker Street. She had the taxi pull in front of the house, as they were simply dropping off the quiche and ringing the hotel to meet Barbier.

"We will give it to Miss Hudson to keep until we get back from the Savoy. We shall all try it. But for now, I would like that bread."

He ripped a piece of the baguette off for her.

At Baker Street, Miss Hudson was most intrigued with the quiche.

They stayed long enough to finish the baguette and ring the Savoy, before heading out once more. This time they used the front door, and Irene made a show of locking the bolt and stretching before climbing into the Vauxhall.

* * * * *

The man behind the counter gave them a funny look as they walked into the hotel for the third time. Irene ignored him and went straight for the restaurant. One of Barbier's men came in after them; from her peripherals, it was the one who'd been parked outside their flat.

Barbier sat at the table at the back, flanked by two large men. At this point, it was getting silly. They were no match for Irene and Joe, their only purpose being to intimidate. She highly doubted they would attack them in the middle of a fancy hotel.

They both sat in front of Barbier as he poured himself a glass of wine.

"We met with both your mother, and your father's mistress," Irene said, feeling Joe stiffen beside her. She had warned him she would be abrupt.

Barbier straightened, dark eyes widening.

"You...what? When did you do this?"

He glanced behind at the large man who was supposed to be watching them. Irene couldn't see his gesture, but it didn't make Andre very happy.

"Why did you not tell me this?" he snapped at them.

"We *are* telling you."

He leaned forward and Irene matched his pose. "Where are they?"

She shrugged and lied to him. "Laverne was on her way out of town, and your mother was at a restaurant finishing her meal. Both of them said they did not touch your father's belongings, at least not to the extent where they would donate them to a museum. Your mother took what she wanted, sold it, then moved on. Miss DuBois said she didn't want anything."

"My mother did it," the Frenchman sat back. "It was her."

Irene hesitated, trying to determine if Barbier had even heard what she'd just said. Joe, probably just as bewildered, set his notebook on the table and tapped his pen.

"Did what?" he asked. "Donate the book?"

"Yes."

Irene shook her head. "I don't believe she did."

"Well, Laverne *wouldn't* have. She has no reason to."

Irene went against her better judgment and let him have a minute. Perhaps he would see the absurdity with which he was speaking. However, he gave a curt nod, doubling down.

She gestured at him. "Why are we having this conversation? Why hire us if you were just going to accuse your mother of everything?"

"Where is she?"

"She was leaving some restaurant."

"Find her."

"You hired us to bring you the person who donated the diary. And we have not found that person yet."

"Then why are you here?"

"To rule out the two people who you think stole your belongings. And to gather more information. Tell us why the estate is inaccessible? Is it because it was burned?"

"Why would it be burned? No. There was a tree that fell right in the middle of it."

Joe scribbled a note. "Why couldn't you have told us that earlier?"

Irene caught the narrowing of Barbier's eyes and recalled a line from his father's diary.

"You knocked the tree into the estate. It was a weak one, and in an attempt to remove it, the trunk fell into the house. Did it kill someone when it fell?"

He turned his sharp eyes to her, not unlike his mother did earlier that day.

"Everyone was given plenty of warning when it fell. My father's butler did not listen and was crushed. Accident. Tragic. I do not like how you came to know about the tree."

Irene was tempted to boast, but kept quiet. The less translations of the diary Barbier thought they did, the better.

"I want to know more about your mother," Irene said, hoping to catch him off guard again.

It worked.

"What about?"

Joe leaned forward and lowered his voice. "We know she wasn't the nicest mother to you—"

"*Silencio!* Where did you hear this?"

"Is it untrue?" Irene asked, keeping calm.

Barbier stared at her for a long moment, then snapped his fingers. All four of his men departed, leaving them in silence.

He finally resigned and dropped most of his bravado. He suddenly looked the twenty-two years of age he was, and yet ten years older at once.

"She was not the nicest. Which is why she donated the books."

"Except she didn't. She thinks the place burnt to the ground."

"Why would she think that?"

Joe glanced at Irene. She had to be careful with her words, lest Barbier think Laverne lied to them. However, this may shed some more light on the mistress.

"Miss Dubois told her as such," Irene said, and under the table, Joe knocked her knee with his own.

Barbier stared at them both. "Of course she did. So, my mother could not take any more things."

Irene wanted to reach across the table and shake the man. He'd turned blind against anyone but his mother. Which meant that unless they dragged that woman to his feet—which Irene wasn't inclined to do—the case was stagnant.

She was sure Laverne was the culprit, but she didn't want to tell Barbier until she knew more. She also had no idea why the mistress would donate such an item, or why she would keep its partner.

The woman had obviously lied for some reason. To protect herself or a loved one, Irene didn't know yet. She needed one more conversation with her.

When neither of them spoke again, Barbier broke the silence. "Is that all you have for me?"

Irene had a million questions for him, but none that would help more than another conversation with Laverne. However…

"If you knew about Miss DuBois, and she was willing to take you in, why not go to her? Why stay with your mother in what sounds like horrid conditions?"

At first, Irene thought he wasn't going to answer, as the man simply stared at her with daggers in his eyes.

"That would disgrace my father," he finally said. "As much as I wanted to, that would not do. Laverne wanted no part of the business, either."

"She couldn't have minded that much. She did stay with your father for years."

Again, he just stared at them for a long moment before speaking. "I feel you are wasting time. Either find the other book, or bring my mother to me and I will figure out where she put it."

Arguing was futile, so Irene stood. "We will be back tomorrow morning, then."

Barbier stood as well, with Joe not a second behind.

"You will be back when you are done this case, even if that is midnight."

Irene didn't answer. She turned on her heel and marched away.

* * * * *

"How are we going to get past the doorman this time?" Joe asked as they parked down the street.

Irene had driven in several circles and taken the long way to Laverne's flat, lest Andre's men were quick to follow them. But she didn't spot any of the black vehicles as they started down the pavement.

"We are simply going to ask to speak with her."

She walked up to Alfred, and he looked her up and down.

"Weren't you here earlier?"

"No. We were not. But I am looking for Laverne DuBois. If you would be so kind…"

He was shaking his head. "She just left, I'm afraid."

"Did she say where she was going?" Irene asked, then softened her voice at the man's quizzical brow. "We were to meet her for dinner."

"She did not."

He offered up no more information, and Irene didn't have the time to waste anymore. She pivoted on her heels and headed back to the car.

Joe mumbled a thank you and hurried after her.

* * * * *

"I assume we're heading to the estate?" Joe said as Irene turned the car toward the outskirts of the city.

"We are. Laverne has the other book, and we do not have the time to hunt her down right now. For all we know, she could've returned to the estate to actually burn it down."

"That would be convenient. But what would we do with her? Are we really going to return that second book to Barbier?"

"Not without translating it first. The diary we possessed held nothing particularly exciting. However, if Laverne is keeping this one, there may be something fascinating in it, which I want to find out."

* * * * *

Irene drove in several circles, with Joe on lookout, to assure no one was following them. They were both prepared for Barbier to show up, though she hoped their words soothed him enough to stay at the hotel and meet them again the next morning.

The only lights shining across the countryside were from the Vauxhall. The laneway was overgrown, as was the large front garden. Just as Barbier described, a downed tree split the west wing of the house from the rest. Bricks lay scattered around the trunk, and a few were stacked, as if someone attempted to clean up the accident.

"It's not burned," Irene muttered.

Joe touched her arm. "Did you see that? A light in the window. First floor, far left."

There were no other vehicles, and no footprints for Irene to look at. Nothing to indicate who rummaged around.

"Laverne?"

Irene shrugged.

The house remained dark as they crept forward. Then, a torch flashed in the window again. A French cuss word came from beyond the broken wall and they both stopped. Whomever was in there was coming out.

Amelia Barbier stumbled over the brick as she climbed the broken wall and exited the house. She saw them and shined her torch on their faces. "Oh, it is you. That woman never burned the place."

"Yes, clearly she was lying." Irene said, glancing at the woman's empty hands. "We told you not to return here."

She snorted. "And I should have listened. There is nothing here, but I had to look. It is a horrible and ugly house. The tree was doing it a favour. There is even a smell coming from it."

She gazed upon the house with such disgust, as if it had personally offended her.

"You really stayed that unhappy for money?" Joe asked.

"The money made me happy. Also, there was a war, and I was an old woman. What was I to do?"

Automobile lights flashed up the laneway as a large, dark car soared toward them. The tires screeched and the passenger door flew open. Andre Barbier climbed out and locked eyes with his mother.

Chapter VIII
More Death at a Dilapidated Estate

"Andre?" Amelia said. "You made it back from the war. Good for you."

Her words didn't need to be spoken. Of course, she knew he was back from the war; Joe and Irene had told her as such. And yet she felt the need to insult him. Her voice was flat, and she made no move to escape her son.

Joe tensed as Barbier looked ready to knock down anyone in his path. The lights from his automobile, and the torches they all held, lit up the four of them, and Joe could just make out the hulking bodyguard back by the vehicles.

"I took over Father's business," Barbier spat at his mother.

"You could never handle your father's business. But I suppose you handled a war."

"Where is Father's other book?"

"The diary? I do not know. I already told them that I do not know. Why would I have it?"

"Liar!"

He said something to her in French.

She answered in the same language, then spoke again in English. "I must go. There is nothing in that house. Goodbye—"

Barbier lifted a revolver, aiming at his mother.

With the torch shining directly on his face, Joe saw just how tired the boy was. He looked like he hadn't slept last night at all and spent the day waiting in the harshly lit restaurant. He looked both like a small boy trying to stand up to his mother, and like a soldier that had seen too many deaths.

The revolver never wavered, despite the angry tremors washing through his body.

Joe glanced at Irene, but she watched with an almost gleeful look. Did it occur to her that Barbier might turn the gun on them once he pulled the trigger? He wanted to signal to her to get back to their vehicle, but she kept her eyes glued to the Frenchman.

Mrs. Barbier was either brave or stupid because she scoffed at her son. "Put that away. Now."

To Joe's surprise, Barbier's hand shook briefly, as if he would listen to her. Like a reflex. Or a soldier taking commands from a superior. The man looked both petrified and enraged all at once. Tears welled in his eyes and a vein in his neck was just visible in the light.

Then, in the distance, tires on gravel and headlights flashed.

Joe took the opportunity to step away, jerking his head to get Irene to do the same. She obeyed and took a few steps sideways.

The car pulled up beside the Vauxhall and Laverne DuBois stepped out. She gasped as she took in the scene. "Oh, my…Andre? What are you doing?"

"What are *you* doing?" Irene snapped.

"I thought that this might happen, so I came here."

Irene and Laverne exchanged some look that Joe didn't understand, and Irene let her pass.

"Andre," the mistress cooed, walking closer to him. "Put the gun down, sweetie."

"Why are you here?" Barbier asked.

"To get you." Laverne's voice remained calm, but she gripped her sleeves. "Come home with me. We can go back to France if you want. I'd love to go back home and see what you've done since the war."

For a moment, Joe thought her words worked, but then Amelia shifted on her feet, bringing Barbier back to life. He drew his attention to her, adjusting his grip on the revolver.

"You are my mother. You were supposed to care for me."

"But she didn't, Andre," Irene said. "Laverne did and still does."

Irene's words were rushed, and almost impatient. Joe knew she didn't think fondly of Amelia at all. Therefore, she didn't care if the woman lived or died. While he understood, he really didn't want to witness yet another death, no matter how deserving.

Barbier didn't listen, he just kept glaring at his mother.

"During the war, I saw mothers take bullets for their children. Stand in front of them as the enemy screamed in their face. I saw the sacrifices they made for their children. And all you did was lock me in the cupboard when I made too much noise. I'm surprised you didn't join the Germans when they came into town."

Joe stepped forward, the talk of war churning his gut. He needed to end this whole thing and go home. "The war hurt us all, and we are all still dealing with the outcome of having to do such brutal things. But it is over now. We can all move on—"

"How?" Barbier snapped, gaze still locked on his mother, like the good soldier he had been. "I have no good memories of before the war. The only thing I was good at was killing Germans and now I have to pretend like it didn't happen? I am supposed to just sell shirts to businessmen and go to the cinema? I do not even know how to do those things. I was never taught to have fun. Because of you."

Joe gestured to Laverne. "You have someone willing to be your family standing right here. She will take you to the cinema. She will make you biscuits."

But Barbier never budged. In fact, he looked calm, like he could pull the trigger and move on with his life. It was a razor's edge. He could fire one bullet or empty the weapon. And Joe didn't want to find out which.

Laverne shuffled forward. "Put the gun down, *mon couer*. Please."

He wasn't listening.

Joe's gut tightened. Andre was going to pull the trigger.

Laverne tried again. "Andre, please—"

The gunshot rang loud and clear through the night.

Mrs. Barbier crumpled to the ground, blood seeping out her back.

Andre dropped his arm, and the gun slipped out of his fingers.

Joe rushed forward and scooped the weapon from the ground, getting it away from the man. His fingers tightened around the revolver as he stood in front of Irene. Though Barbier had no weapon, he still looked dark and dangerous.

Irene grabbed Laverne's bag, attempting to drag her away. The purse slipped from the woman's arm, but she stumbled back to them.

As if someone pulled a switch, Barbier straightened and headed toward the ruins of the estate. He stepped over his dead mother, avoiding the blood.

Irene handed Laverne her bag, then called out.

"Andre!" She went after him before Joe could grab her.

As Barbier turned to her, she held out a yellow leather-bound book.

Beside Joe, Laverne gasped and looked through her bag.

Irene had taken the book, Joe realized. Stolen it from the woman to give to Barbier.

As the man took the book from Irene, she spoke. "I've learned that not all mothers are meant to bear children. Yours and mine are one and the same. Take this, find whatever peace you need in this house, then get out of my city."

He stared at the book. "Who—"

"The case is done and we shall take our leave. The police may or may not be here in a few hours. Use that information to your advantage."

"I have no plans on ever returning to the city. And I hope to never see you again."

"Likewise."

He called to Joe. "Doctor, thank your service, and hopefully our countries don't have to fight side by side again."

Joe gave him a nod, but kept a tight grip on the pistol. Barbier appeared calm, but his eyes were wide and full of anger still, just like the soldiers during the war. Half of them here and present, the other half far away, as if they were trying to forget everything they saw as it was happening.

The man glanced at Laverne, who still clutched her purse. He headed toward his automobile and opened the passenger door for her, waiting. Laverne went to step forward, but Irene grabbed her.

"You are lucky I took that diary before Andre found it." She kept her voice low and spoke quick. "What was recorded in it?"

"Francois's personal accounts. Of how he and I met, and how he felt about Andre. No admission of crimes, just a story of love."

"If he ever finds out you donated that other diary—"

"He shall never find out. He doesn't need to follow in his father's footsteps, and I was trying to ensure he didn't. But that's all for naught, isn't it?"

"He needs help," Joe said. "He needs to speak to someone about everything that has happened to him."

"That will not happen, Doctor. But perhaps one day he will write his own diary. Thank you for your help."

"Be careful," Irene said. "He is an unstable man."

"He just needs someone to love him like the son he never was." She glanced once more at Amelia's body before joining Andre.

"I don't know if she is a dumb woman or a brave one," Irene said. "Becoming the mistress to a powerful criminal, and then a mother-figure to a dangerous and unstable one?"

Joe shrugged, ears still ringing. "I have no idea what to make of the situation."

He was still in disbelief that a mother would mistreat their own child to a point where she got killed for it. He knew some parents were cruel, but to see that play out didn't register quite yet.

"What do we do with her?" He asked.

"Andre's men will assumingly take care of the body. But I do believe we are done. I don't expect him to cause us any more trouble. He didn't even want to in the first place. He just wanted revenge."

Joe looked at the gun still in his hand.

"Toss that," Irene instructed. "Let his men take care of it, too. But wipe it first. And you'll need to scrub your hands."

He had been ready to pull the trigger and defend Irene with his life.

He was always ready to defend her, of course. But he'd never had to do it with a weapon in his hand. Would he have pulled the trigger?

Undoubtedly, yes.

His stomach churned as he tossed the weapon to the ground.

As they climbed into the Vauxhall, a large vehicle pulled up to the body and four men exited. Irene drove away, and neither of them looked back.

* * * * *

"How am I going to put any of this into a report?" DI Lestrade pinched the bridge of his nose as Joe and Irene sat across from him in his office.

"Perhaps you don't," Irene said. "It's the business of the French gangsters, now."

"You know how ridiculous that sounds, right? How outlandish?"

"Yes. But it's also the classic tale of revenge."

"We can give our statements," Joe offered. "We can help, but there is nothing to find."

"There are the men who buried the body. There's Mr. Barbier himself," Lestrade pointed out.

Irene shrugged. "I would leave it, Eddy. We were simply here to tell you we've wrapped up the case and we can all move on."

"This will not come back to me in any way?" he asked, then groaned. "Now *I* sound like the gangster."

"Oh Eddy. No one would mistake you for a criminal."

"Thank you, I suppose. Well, let me know if anything else happens. And bid your sisters farewell for me. Marla loved having them visit, though the smaller one, Alice, wasn't as keen."

They all stood, and Joe shook the DI's hand. "Thank you again. I owe you."

"Don't be daft. You owe me nothing."

* * * * *

"Why can't we stay longer?" Alice stomped her foot as they stood at the train station the following morning, luggage in hand.

"Because you have school and Mum and Dad are expecting you home." Joe did up an extra button on her coat to keep the wind out. "You will come back soon, I promise."

"Ireeeene," she pouted. "Can we stay? I don't need school."

"Ha!" Irene said. "You do, Alice. At least for right now, as your handwriting leaves much to be desired and you must learn to quit stomping your foot. But next time you visit, we'll do all the things we promised and you can come to the morgue with me."

"Irene," Joe exclaimed over Alice's excited gasp.

"Eleanor," she ignored Joe and his sister, turning to the older girl. "Be smart and be bold. Next time I see you, I expect no silly nonsense."

Joe tensed, as he knew Eleanor wouldn't take any of those words kindly. However, to his complete surprise, his sister nodded as if given the most important task.

Joe hugged them both and blinked back tears. He wasn't sure if Irene noticed, or simply needed to comfort herself, but as the train chugged away and his sisters waved out the window, she wrapped her hands around his arm. That gesture threatened to bring out even more tears, but he hugged her closer to his body.

The past two days had been full of anger and frustration, and he missed his sisters dearly. However, as he stood on the platform, watching the last car of the train turn round the bend, he realised the progress that Irene had made. She had empathy and had learned when to apologise, and knew when his mood was off.

And in turn, he felt he was finally allowed to be angry and frustrated without having to tiptoe around his feelings.

He was probably thinking way too much about everything and he simply needed a nap, but it felt like a further step in their relationship.

Or friendship.

Or whatever it was they had between them.

Chapter IX

Outlandish Thoughts About the Future

After returning home from the train station, Joe carried down the box of things his sisters had brought with them from his parents.

"I will get to this box when I return from Sarah's."

Irene waved him off. She had photos and files to sort from this case, after all. Eddie had rung them just before Joe left, letting them know that he did sent some constables out to the estate. No bodies were found. However, a few small fires lit in the interior, and most of the place was burned to a crisp.

Irene was not surprised in the least. Shooting one's mum was quite harsh, but there was a large part of her that knew exactly where Andre's feelings lay.

An hour after she started her sorting, she stood from the couch in need of a bigger area for her papers. She turned to the table, then sighed. Joe's things from his mother sat in the middle.

Irene dumped the photographs onto the sofa and collected Joe's box. Inside, a small container slid out from under some letters and caught her eye. It was dark blue leather and looked a bit worn, but well taken care of.

She swiped it and opened the lid. Inside was a diamond and gold ring.

Irene stared at it for a solid half-minute, like a magpie catching a shiny object. She'd always been inclined to like very specific jewellery, and could never figure out why certain pieces caught her eye, but this did. The diamonds were symmetrical and pleasing to the eye. The band was thick and sturdy for a working woman's hand, and yet delicate enough to make even the most gnarled and worked fingers seem dainty.

She plucked it from the velvet and held it to the light.

Oh, yes, this ring was quite lovely, and…

It settled onto her hand as if made for it.

She stared at her left hand, the ring sparkling in the kitchen light. Her stomach tightened and heat pooled behind her ears.

Why did she enjoy the look of this jewellery on her hand? This specific piece, to be exact. It should have felt, and looked, out of place.

It didn't belong to her, though, and it shouldn't be on her finger. That feeling battled with the urge to keep it on forever.

Before her stomach completely imploded, she stuck the ring back in the box.

* * * * *

By the time Joe returned, she'd sorted their case and cleared off the board, ready for the next one. She sat on the couch, doing today's crossword as he removed his jacket and boots.

"We have a package from France. Sent express."

She put her puzzle down and joined him in the kitchen. The box was neat, not a mark on it, and tied together with a bow.

"What if it's a bomb, or something dangerous?"

"Look at the bow," Irene said. "That's a professional knot if I've ever seen one."

She opened the box. Two matching deep green wool coats, one a ladies cut, the other a man's, sat folded next to each other. Irene recognised the designer name, only because she'd seen it on the coats and dresses the rich ladies wore from their case last year involving beautiful red dogs.

By this time, Joe had retrieved a note from the bottom of the box:

Dr and Mrs Holmes,

Thank you for your assistance. It was greatly appreciated. I will never be back in London, but you both have an open invitation to a lunch in Paris.

Merci,

AB

"Didn't want to use his real name, I guess," Joe mumbled, looking over his jacket.

Irene saw the signature and started laughing. "Another AB for the books."

Joe shook his head.

They both pulled on the jackets and they fit like a glove. Joe's made him appear even taller and drew out the colour in his dark auburn hair and blue eyes.

He looked at Irene and smiled. "That does look quite fetching on you, especially with your short hair."

"It is very warm and feels so very nice. I believe we shall keep these coats."

She took hers off and flung it over the chair. As nice as the gift was, it wasn't cold enough to wear it outside yet, and she had a crossword puzzle to finish.

Just as she settled back on the couch, Joe cleared his throat.

"Uh, Irene?"

"Hm?"

"Where are my mother's things?"

She nudged the box beside her as she filled out an answer.

Joe mumbled something under his breath and retrieved it from the couch. She heard him rummage through it before pausing.

"Did you go through this box?"

"Would there be anything of interest to me?"

"Only belongings of mine."

She waved him off. "There isn't a lot I don't know about you, Joe. Though, if you ever plan on giving that ring to someone, they must have larger fingers, at least a size eight."

"So, you *did* go through the box."

She shrugged and filled in yet another answer. "I am an investigator. It is my job to know things."

"You tried it on, didn't you?"

"Yes, and it fit perfectly on my size eight finger."

He sighed, but instead of his usual exasperated noises, which Irene knew all too well, this was one filled with apprehension and sadness. "That's good to know, I suppose."

"Sarah's fingers are much slimmer," she said, trying to deflect. "And her knuckles are slender. You'd probably need to size down if you plan on giving it to her. Or buy a new ring altogether."

"I don't want to buy a new ring. The point is to give this one to someone."

"Then you need to find someone with larger hands."

He left the box on the table and sat across from her.

"You know," he said, then held up his hands as she glared at him for interrupting her puzzle. "This will be quick, I promise. You were different than I expected with my sisters, but you were quite good with them."

"Thank you. Older children are far easier than younger ones. Well, to speak with anyway. I suppose babies, being babies, only babble and eat and burp. It's when they begin to talk until they are Alice's age that I find difficult. They don't understand anything, yet they want to know everything and walk away as you try to explain things."

Joe raised a brow. "So, you're saying you would do well with a small baby?"

She put her crossword down. "I suppose. Well, maybe not. I don't know. I haven't been around enough children. And who knows if I will have any of my own?"

"You've mentioned you don't want children," he said, a slight hesitation in his voice, as if treading into unknown territory.

Irene simply shrugged. "Knowing me and my habits, I'd be inclined to mess up their childhood. Or that there would be days where they would bother me, or that…" She trailed off, serious thoughts suddenly pounding her mind. "I just don't know if I could love them how children should be loved."

As soon as she spoke, regret swooped over her. What a silly statement to say aloud. Certain social cues went over her head, but surely that was a sentence best kept in one's mind.

"Oh, Irene. I think if you're worried about that sort of thing, then you're already halfway to being a great mum."

Joe smiled at her, the kind he only saved when she said something he found both silly and endearing. It made her squirm every time because it was a reminder that he cared for her.

She laughed, trying to deflect again. "Can you imagine me with a big pregnant belly waddling around 221b? I'd eat everything in sight and knock over everything in my path."

Joe laughed along with her, then paused and gave her that smile again. "Funny enough, I can."

She looked at her bedroom, trying to keep the mood light, though she knew she was failing horribly. "That would have to be the baby's room. And I'd have to share your room. We'd need a bigger bed to fit both of us, of course."

Joe sat back in the chair. "Ah, right, I forgot that you're never letting me leave Baker Street."

"If you leave, who is going to help me with the baby?"

"The father?"

"I forgot about that."

Joe laughed. "It's a pretty important part. Whoever it is should be so honoured."

Irene snorted. "So they should."

She tried to go back to her puzzle, but her mind was completely distracted, which rarely happened. Though it was becoming more commonplace these days as she became more social and thought about life outside Baker Street.

"My father met my mother while working undercover for a criminal organisation," she said, expecting the familiar tenseness in her belly that came about when speaking about her father. Surprisingly, though, none came, and she kept speaking as Joe gave her his full attention. "He was chasing a rather dangerous criminal. In order to get closer, he had to commit to a relationship with my mother. And when you commit to someone, sometimes a baby occurs."

As she finished her story, that feeling came upon her. Anxious, heated worry. Why was she telling this to Joe? What insight was she hoping to gain by revealing how she was made?

He didn't appear to be judging or expecting anything more, and he certainly wasn't looking down upon her father, either. Not that he would at all. But she didn't know what to expect.

"What happened once her parents found out? Were they the criminals he was hunting?"

Irene shrugged. She could stop the story right now, and Joe wouldn't say a word. But a part of her needed to keep going.

"They were on the outskirts, so he never told them he was a private detective. He just made them believe he was a vagrant passing through. He never went into greater details than that, but her parents weren't too happy and didn't even want a grandchild either. So, they offered my father a hefty sum to take me away and never return. Of course, my mother returned several years later and demanded me back and my father sent her away again."

"Did he take the money? From what I've heard about him, I wouldn't think of him as a type to be bought off."

Irene smiled despite herself, remembering how her father told the story. He had smiled at her and said, 'Dear child, I took every penny and pound and sprinkled it all on you.' Then he'd handed ten-year-old Irene a five-pound note to spend.

"Uncle John told me once that the only reason he took the money was to teach them a lesson and to spoil me. It wasn't until years later they found out who he truly was and by that time the criminals he was hunting were all dead or locked away."

"I don't remember reading about any of that."

"Oh, no. He made my uncle swear to never record it."

She put her crossword down, completely distracted and hungry for tea. She couldn't look at Joe, as feelings brimmed at the surface, and if she looked into his kind, caring eyes, those feelings might overflow.

However, she still had more words about her father to get out of her mind. She thought of a parent's love—or the love they were supposed to have for their children—and how this past case wasn't the first time they'd run across a parent who was unhappy with the fact that they had children. The thoughts sat sour in her mouth and she had to speak to release them.

"Father said to me once that as soon as he saw me, he knew that he loved me and would give his last breath for me. Imagine knowing so easily how you care about, or love, someone? It seems ridiculous, something so huge for some people, and that come so easily to them."

"It's feelings," Joe offered. "We are not in charge of them."

She looked at him and raised a brow. "That is the most ridiculous thing you have ever said."

He snorted. "Tell me one person who is in complete control of their feelings. Not even you are."

"I am offended."

Joe smiled at her with that look she hadn't seen him give anyone else. She squirmed.

"Okay, fine. I wish I was in charge of my feelings. Life would be a lot easier."

Joe sighed. "Yes, it would."

She felt his eyes on her, which wasn't entirely odd, however, this time he looked like he wanted to say a thousand words.

He blinked suddenly, then stood. "I'm running out of room in the notebook you gave me. I think I'll pop to the shop and get a new one."

He spoke quickly, clearly nervous. Irene hated when he didn't say what he actually wanted to, as she could never figure out what he truly meant, and he never ended up telling her.

"Are you going to wear your new coat?"

"No, I think I shall save that for when you and I are on a case."

"The keys to the auto are in my bag."

"Oh, I was going to walk."

"Suit yourself. I'll have Miss Hudson hold off tea for you."

He left in a hurry, and she stood and went to the window. He exited the building and stopped on the pavement, running his hand through his hair. He looked up and down the street, as if he didn't know where to go.

He'd been doing more of that lately—the leaving to walk aimlessly—and it frustrated her to no end because she couldn't figure out why. They used to joke all the time, but recently he'd turn melancholy, or his face would redden if a sensitive subject was brought up.

She knew things between him and Sarah were not the best—whatever their best was—so perhaps joking about the future or serious relationships, or happiness, reminded him of the work he still had to do with her.

Irene sighed.

Relationships, in general, were a lot to ponder. Perhaps she truly had no idea if they were supposed to take that much work, but she didn't think so.

If only it were acceptable for her and Joe to live together forever, even start a family, without having to marry or have a relationship…

But, alas, that was a dream for another day, as she had better things to think about right now. She didn't know what, but there had to be something. Perhaps she'd figure out how to curl her hair after it's already been curled. Or perhaps she and Isla would take a nap and wait for Joe to return from the shops.

As if the dog could read her mind, she whined up at Irene.

"I agree. Come, Isla. Let's nap until Joe comes home."

The two of them wandered into Irene's bedroom, ready to sleep away the afternoon.

The end

Holmes & Co. will return in:

Return to Baskerville

Christmas is only a few weeks away at 221b Baker Street! As Irene sets up the decorations, a jovial man name Mr. Dearborn asks for her assistance with a strange request. He's purchased the famous Baskerville Hall, and he is determined to have Irene and Joe assure him that there is not, in fact, a giant hound that roams the grounds. She refuses at first until he hands over a sum of money unlike Irene has ever seen.

Once Irene and Joe arrive at Baskerville, not all is what it seems. Dearborn confesses he is a fanatic of the Sherlock Holmes stories and demands to know more about the elusive detective now that he has his daughter in his grasp. He also surprises Irene and Joe — and the other guests he failed to mention — with a re-enactment of the story of the Hound of the Baskervilles, with the pair taking centre stage. Now in the middle of the most well-known Sherlock Holmes story of them all, Irene and Joe must outsmart, and out fight a man who thinks he knows more about Sherlock than they do.

About the Author

Allison Osborne lives in Ontario, Canada with her son, their rabbits, and an overwhelming amount of vintage trinkets. When her mind isn't wandering through 1940s England, she's busy dabbling in scriptwriting and other grand adventures.

Connect with Allison:

Instagram: @allisonoauthor

Website: www.aosborneauthor.com

www.ingramcontent.com/pod-product-compliance
Ingram Content Group UK Ltd.
Pitfield, Milton Keynes, MK11 3LW, UK
UKHW020151020925
462463UK00006BA/87